Love's Gathering

Emotions From The Heart

By

Heartsender

14 NOV 2003

TO YVONNE,

My ATRC shipmate, This book is a reflection or The Beauty one can possess. I hope you find the beauty it hides in the depth of each poem.

Homer
AKA Heart-sender

ISBN: 0-7596-9051-0

This book is printed on acid free paper.

Cover Design By
Patricia Hunke

Edited By
Greer O'Bryant
And
Tom Short

1stBooks - rev. 5/13/02

In Memory of

Aunt Gloria

November 9, 1939 - January 21, 2002

DEDICATION

Mom and Dad - who raised nine inspirational kids

Rhashida, Annette, Tierita, Angela (YaYa), Marnita, and Holly my twin - My six beautiful sisters who instilled in me the value of women

Christopher and Michael - My brothers who I look up to.

Channing - my son who I live for.

Mychal - my son that I never knew

Margo - The Heart and friend that inspired most of my poetry from around the world

Asami - My lifetime friend who will always be there

Aunt Dorothy - my newly found Aunt

Allison, Cathy, and Karen - who will always be a part of me

PREFACE

I am the HeartSender in true form
With words that will calm
Any soul's crazy tempered storm
I am sometimes called The Heart
Reaching deep into your thoughts
Tearing your chaotic world all apart
Making you see into your own fantasy
As you get lost in dreams
Away from all you know as reality
I give you stories and sometimes rhymes
As you vision yourself
Lost for all of time
I show you love as it is known
Giving you a warm sensation
You can finally call your own
I give you happiness and tears to embrace
Showing you both sides of emotions
In life's unending Heart throbbing race
The Heart knows what you are going through
Whether it is the finding of love
Or losing a love that was true
So sit back and relax
And receive this mind massage
That will have your world dancing
To the melody of life's fainting mirage
As your HeartSender I will make your Heart sing
As you witness this Heart
Experiencing Love's Gathering

CONTENTS

xi

March 20, 2000

<u>SUNSET</u>

Your eyes, filled with smoke
Of drowning fire.
Every single moment
Stored in tears
Of coming waves,
Hits the rocks
Of our destiny.
Clouds, unknown lands
Just dying to be discovered.
Sky of mystery,
Moment of silence,
And
The end...Is it?

DREAMING OF LOVE

Dreaming of love is easy
Before I go to bed tonight
I will think of her
The woman I have never seen
The woman that is my destiny
I will think of all the things
I always wanted to tell her
I will tell her of my childhood dreams
I will tell her of my fantasies
I will tell her of my fears
I will tell her of my heartbreaks
I will tell her about my family
And then in her arms, I will shed only one
tear
To show my love
I will then think of ways
I wanted to love her
I will think of slowly undressing her
As my stare
Into her eyes
Remain locked
I will look deep into her soul
As I slowly reveal each bare breast
And each tender thigh
She possess
And then I will tell her
To undress me
As she uncovers
The curves of muscles
In my chest
As the tattoo comes to life
As she reveals
The essence of my manhood
And then watches it come to life
As the veins
Becomes vessels of love
And then I will slowly touch her
Nice and softly
First upon her rosey cheeks

Then upon the soft curves
Of her shoulders and arms
Then upon the Heartstopping cushions
Of her right breast
Watching the nipples harden
Then I will venture onto the left breast
As the nipple fights for life
I will then take her hands
And place them
Upon my chest
As she sculptures
The strength I possess
I will then take her left hand
And slowly guide it to a new life
Down to my nature
As she feels
The vessels of love
Float upon a dream
I will then pull her to me
As her stiffened nipples
Press against the walls of my chest
Then I will kiss her
I will kiss away the sleepless nights
I will kiss away the loneliness
I will kiss away the tears
I will kiss into her my love
So deeply
So true
Then I will lift her
Into my arms
Into the arms of a man
That has no boundaries
Of love for a woman
I will carry her
To the bed
And slowly place her down
Then kiss her once more
Kissing down to each breast
As my tongue circles
Each now bursting nipple
Bringing a roll to her hips
I will then kiss her down further

To the naval
Tasting the sweat
Then down south further
Debating on if I shall ever return
For once I taste the treasure
My greed may never cease
My tongue then dances
Upon each thigh
As she spreads
Her legs even more
Grasping my head
Pleading for more
My tongue then finds
What the venture promised
It entered so slowly
And comforting
I will taste all she had
I will taste her fruits
As her body will roll
To the beat of my tongue
I could hear her moans
Wanting more
Pleading for more
Over and over
And Over again
Hours go by
And yet I am still tasting her
Then finally
I rise
Spreading apart
Her juicy legs
Then I slowly enter
With ease
Stroke after stroke
I will give my loving
Again and again
Deeper and deeper
Kissing her
With all I have
Thinking of her
Thinking of how much
I truly love her

Not wanting to stop
But faster and faster
And faster I go
In and out
In and out
Her nails
Give pain to my back
And the deeper I go
God! Don't let it end
Again and again
Please!
Please!
No!
No!!!
I love you!!!
Damn I love you!
Again and again
Faster then faster
Deeper and Deeper
Then
I could feel the juices
Inside of her increase
Causing my release
Oh the feeling.
Of her orgasm
The feeling of being within
Then slower and slower
Then slowly we kiss
We kiss so deeply
And I can see the tears
Come down her face
And the smile she possessed
Letting me know
Those were happy tears
And finally she spoke
And she said:
"I love you"
And I knew
That I will never
Love anyone else
Ever again
And my dreaming of Love

5

Heartsender

    Will be only dreams
    Of Loving only her
    My destiny woman

April 27, 1999

DESERT GOLD

Rolling away from me I can see
The Desert Gold dancing for me.
No glitter, no shine to melt away
The endless plain cooling the day.
Ripple be one of a colony
Seeking the heated majesty.
Glimmer before the departing sun
Through these eyes looking into one.
I smile entranced about my stern
To the leaping of whales to burn.
Up to the stars my stare dare glance
Not to miss the Desert Gold's last dance.

April 22, 1999

ONE POSSESSION

A simple picture would STILL me away
Like many days at SEE.
I often ONE DER what comes TWO day
To part with all EYE have - - M TEE.

November 07, 2000

<u>TEARS</u>

They say that a man
Is not suppose to cry
But who ever made that rule
Has not had love pass them by

Yes I cry, night after night
From the lost memories
Of how I held her body tight

You will see it yourself
Those fatal running tears
Once the hurt inside
Awaitingly appears

The long walks I take
To hopefully forget
Does me no good-
My Heart faithfully admits

Its funny how the tears
Come with no end
For love is a painful game
You can never ever win

So don't hold back my friend
Let the tears come at will
And be a man who knows
How losing true love feels

<u>CRAZY</u>

Voices in my head
Whispers to me each day
When ever the moon sets
Or when she passes my way

Lolli pops?
No french vanilla!!
Is what I now crave
Oh the warnings
As my Heart attempts to misbehave

I take a step
Then eagerly take back two
As lions or tigers
Love as lovers do

I see the night light
Capture my random gaze
But suddenly I cry out her name
As I wonder through this worldly maze

I take a seat
Feeling all eyes are on me
Wanting to taste her tears
Or harvest my sanity

Three, two, one
My breath slowly exhales
As I realize she has me
Under a wicked love spell

I go to a pay phone
Not knowing who to call
As the phone rings
I stare- standing proud and tall

It is for me!!!
Admits the gold in my eye
Yes, this time I know
Love will finally fail to pass me by

But why do I let it ring
Over and over and over again?
Because I fear this time
I just might find love in the end.

November 4, 2000

SIDE BY SIDE

Today as Whitney sung aloud
Her most famous song
I sat side by side
Two lovers whose Hearts
Could do no wrong

He ordered for her
An omelet with no salt
And she ordered for him
What the many years
Has gracefully taught

Oh how the jealousy in me
Was building up inside
As the wrinkles in their smiles
And the familiar glances
Refused to run and hide

Will that be me
In the many years to come
Or will I be another old man
With grandkids, money, and a dog
Yet terribly lonesome

I must have heard
The word "Dear"
To no irritable end
As their conversation flowed
From the love in the air
They both did send

As he grabbed his coat
Then reached for her tender hand
I knew then that in all of my life
I want to find the same love
Across this promising land.

November 5, 2000

ENDLESS WAVES

Under the crescent moon
They flowed as one
Rippling
Splashing
So free
So gentle
Oh how I wanted to be a wave
Traveling from the dept
Of the deep blue ocean
Images of broken clouds
Could not take my eyes
Off the gathering
Of endless waves

The sands-
Reaching for a touch
To be taken away
From its home
Out into a new life
A new freedom
And still they flowed
Again and Again
From the soft western wind
But which wave will I be?
And how far will I travel?
I will have a place
To one day begin
But as in life
I will also have a place
To one day end
Or just start anew
Once upon the sand
To take it to its new life
I will flow again
Back out among the waves
To finally become my dream—
The endless wave

March 23, 1999

CAN'T WAIT

Can't wait to see your beautiful smile
Can't wait to feel the way you make me feel.
Can't wait to go that extra mile
Can't wait to hold you for a moment.
Can't wait see your exotic eyes
Can't wait to dance the night away.
Can't wait to behold your sweet embrace
Can't wait to make you feel the way I do.
Can't wait to see the wonderful sites
Can't wait to be the man I want to be.

March 31, 1999

EMBRACE

Confused and enlightened I sit and wonder
Searching for an explanation to this madness.
What will come in the upcoming moments?
Will I ever know the compassion of the promised eyes?

To my amazement - she smiles at me.
Lifting a hazed mist before my soul

Time stands still as hours pass quickly by
Whispers in the wind fade slowly away.
I laugh to find no ears to hear my cry.
Tears fall to an enchanting beat.

We kiss away the memories not yet known
The moonlight attacks the quicken sweat.
Howls of desire dance the forbidden cry.

What makes this one so special?
How could I replace such a mood?

My life spills away among a lost touch.
All ends to the sorrow prophecy.
With eyes into eyes we embrace.

FAIRLADY

FAIRLADY
  FAIR LADY
    FA IR LA DY!
HENCE THE CRY OF THE BROKEN LAMB.

FAIRLADY
  FAIR LADY
    FA IR LA DY!
THE TEARS ARE DRY ON THE SUNLIT PLAIN

FAIRLADY
  FAIR LADY
    FA IR LA DY!

April 19, 1999

MIDNIGHT

Passing by the Midnight Hour
Leads my heart abandoned and astray.
Denied the promised taste of sour
And the smell of the once gifted flower
To covet the loss of a mourning yesterday.

Not quite dawn to hold this memory true
I fight away my forbidden desire
To feel her tears and frozen fire
All is not red around the circle of blue.

Once her glance embraced all of me.
From time to time it passes me by
Misleading me around for eternity.

I did smell the promised scent of this flower
And danced the song of love this Midnight Hour.

April 25, 1978

WHO AM I?

Who am I?
I shall try to find out until I die.
I will like to know where I am placed
So everyone can see my true face.
I will like to have a family
And place them so the whole world can see
I would like to have a mother who cares
And a father who will always be there
I will like to have a sister who shares
And a brother who plays fair.
I know that I am a special guy
Because God makes the weakest bird fly
So who am I?

April 29, 1999

TOMORROW

The picture was old almost new
From the tear drop stains of Yesterday.
The camera lost ten miles or two
Near the arranged visit of Yesterday.
Son of mine he will always be
In my defense of Yesterday.
Denied all dreams and sanity
Returning home of Yesterday.
Bond be weak in stolen Heart
Surviving the streets of Yesterday.
Living next door and miles apart
Pretending the role of Yesterday.
Sailing off and far away
Becoming my dad of Yesterday.

DIALOG

Sirens screamed down the deserted expressway at this dark snow lit hour. A little boy barely over a year old holds the hand of the only familiar passenger. This passenger was lying down in pain with no comfort from the heat he felt on his chest and the left half of his face. The little boy had no tears in his eyes, just confusion. Why was his dad in pain? There was no fire. The other passenger was someone he had just met a hundred miles ago in a McDonald's restaurant down the street from where his mom dwelled. This passenger was beautiful but far from glamorous. Her skin glowed with the passion of an African Queen as her hair fell just below her neck. Her eyes were sharply brown that pierced any soul that had the pleasure to take a short glimpse. She was a frail slender young vibrant woman whom any man would be proud to claim. Her name was Karen. She was a spawn from the Virgin Islands with an attitude that exploded. But you can clearly see her love for the man in pain. Her eyes were watery as she tightly held his other hand. Was she to blame for his father's pain? Who was this woman to the familiar face? The little boy barely resembled the man in pain with the exception of certain facial features. Their skin complexions were far from a match yet they bonded like father and son.

To wake in pain every night was the curse I felt for eight years. Eight long years of never knowing what could have become of my life if I would have never let her go. Funny how a man finds out how much he loves someone after she has vanished from his life. Regret is what he must live with and sorrow is what he must face day after day. Time was the enemy as the pain never left. They say the Heart would mend after time. But this Heart never has and never will mend. We have a son together and we had a love together. The fool I was made to be and the fool I will always

remain. There will be others, true, but never another
_____ and never another love as the one we shared.
She is now with another. I can lie and claim to be
happy for them and my son. I can lie and wish them
all the happiness in the world. Eight years is a long
time to want someone with all of your Heart. To the
ones that I used or never could devote all of myself-
sorry. What will I do now that she is his? What will
I do? How could I find happiness in the Melody from
the Smile?

June 6, 1999

<u>MELODY IN A SMILE</u>

And I just sat across from an empty phone
—The better part of me
Spilled the water from his lips—
My son with news
—The music stopped playing
Life spilled away into the crawling smile
I could not see where it went
All of me shook
Nothing could—Nothing would—
What am I thinking of?
Why do I cry a lonely melody
TIME is my ENEMY
It fills me with false hopes
The pain STILL stands
Magnified over and over and over
Just one pause
Time out!!!!
Let this smile be real
The white blaze of fire
The water ran around
Her smile enchants me still
The soft song in my ear
For a moment the pain is gone
From the memory
My eyes open
Night falls
No light to guide me to sleep
I lay in the dark
On a bed of ill tears
She is out of my life
No more hoping
No more dreaming
Her hand is his
The silence is golden
The melody in a smile

DIALOG

Ever wondered why things are the way they are? I do, too many times. Just the other day I walked around in a circle looking up at the sky. What if I was the sky? Would I be looking down at the person walking around in a circle or would I have all my attention on that big open dark space and be wondering what's out there? Strange, the curiosity. Thoughts such as these often pass through my mind. Especially when I am with someone special. I don't walk around in a circle thinking about the sky. I simply often think,"What's out there"? Strange, the confusion. These words are not meant to confuse you. Simply to adjust you into the train of thought I often go through. Many nights I find myself in these thoughts. I believe it was sometime last week when I was reading a Stephen King epic- I believe it was 'The Stand'. Of course I did not get a chance to finish reading it. Come on! That book is over a thousand pages. As exciting as it was, my attention kept drifting to my own imagination such as what lies beyond the sky. The only thing I did get from his book was that every great book is made one word at a time. Which is true. Just like now as I sit at my laptop computer at sea onboard the USS Laboon(DDG 58) and typing my thoughts one word at a time. Now my emotions are not so strong because of a long stressful day. I do regret missing my son's birthday yesterday. My son- another long drawn out emotional dramatized situation which I can create endless poetry that could bring tears to my own eyes. I am now wondering if I should stop creating short dialog in between my poems. But I just want to try something different. I am not trying to explain my poetry yet I am trying to make it easier for you to bring yourself into my imagination. Closer and more personal. That is the reason 'Love's Gathering' was created.

August 2, 1999

BROWN SPARROW

Sometimes I wish you were here
    Brown Sparrow
Tending to my wishes.
Sometimes I wish you were far away
For even this strong man
Is weak on one knee before thee.

My Brown Sparrow—
You soar with my Heart
    Upon brown golden wings.
The imprint of your vision
Is forever my savior and enemy.

With two hands and two feet—
    I am a man.
With two lips and two Hearts—
    I am free.
Free to soar with a simple kiss—
Free to glide into your embrace.

Brown Sparrow—
Fly! Fly! Fly!
Fly with your heart
—And love me.

September 14, 1999

FRAGILE THINGS

So easily a Heart is broken
Even if it is your own
A dropped tear
   Such an unpleasant site
So many tears to see.

So easily a promise is broken
Being the sailor that I am
A change of plans
   To break the Heart
So many Hearts to break.

June 27, 1999

THE DANCER

I've danced in places
   most will only see in dreams.
I've danced in ways that
   would satisfy the lonely souls
And in my dance
   I freed my inner thoughts.
So many steps to take
   chance by chance
Even in the darkness
   of the closed outside.

Dezi was my first dance
   -an innocent age-
My steps were clumsy.
No more dancing for this boy
   -I tried to tell myself.
The years past by or so it seemed-
   Hope was my next waltz
Then came Twista and Dezere
   Slow down to the music!!!

As years past
   and the music changed
I danced to only one song
   with _____
I learned new steps, new emotions
   taking me to a higher level
But I continued to dance on
   next with _____
She nearly took the dance away
Forgotten steps and introductions
   led me to _____

Sweet _____
   As _____ shared
I was first to dance with
My rhythm strayed away
   along with the memories.
Then I realized that I was
   A dancer

FORBIDDEN DESIRE

Sweat I taste
Upon her naval
Moans I hear
She faithfully utters
Her desire
Her need
Her wants I must please
Hold up this canvas
As I paint this picture
Into the night
Into her realm
Into her forbidden desire
The hours pass slowly by
As she shakes
Over and Over
And Over again
Bursts of pleasure
Bursts of ecstasy
Floats upon her
Oh how sweet
We flow as one
One beat of the Heart
Two Hearts in one beat
The feel of her breast
The feel of her thighs
The feel of her treasure
Never again will I forget
Never again will I try to remember
Instead I will re-enact
Over and over
And Over again
Just this night
Away from reality
Her forbidden desire
I prey in the shadows
Am I mad!!
Should I stop?
Again I am lost

Again she tastes my neck
Again her nails
Give pain to my back
A pain that forces
A deeper thrust
Over and over
and Over again
Over and over
And Over again
Her lips I tease
Her tongue I please
As it sinks into my ear
Satisfying my every need
Pushing me deeper
Making my muscles tighter
As her love muscles do the same
Over and Over
and Over again
One stride
Upon this ride
Faster
Then faster
Then even faster
As I near the end
Faster
Then faster
Then even faster
As we both reach that point
Faster
Then faster
Then even faster
As our bodies collide
As the sweat pours
Upon the satin sheets
As night is awakened
As howls of desire
Emerge from us both
Faster
Then faster
Then suddenly it is slowed
Then suddenly we again shake
Then suddenly our muscles tighten

Then suddenly we kissed
We kissed away the past
We kissed away the night
We kissed away lost promises
We kissed away the tears
Slower
Then slower
Then even slower
As I am still within her treasure
Slower
Then slower
Then even slower
As my hands re-touched
The parts of her I claimed
Slower
Then slower
Then even slower
As the night
Becomes the day
Over and over
And Over again
Wanting her
Wanting her now
Wanting her then
Wanting her forbidden desire.

CAN LOVE LAST?

Can love last?
I say no!!!
Believe me young fool
I've tried love too many times
Too many times love failed I
Love failed I!!!

Can love last?
I say no!!!
Just yesterday
In my Heart love dwelled
Or so I thought to stay
In the blink of an eye
For me, Love ran away!@#%*!

Can love last?
I say no!!!
For a moment
It floods you with happiness
But for eternity
It embraces you with Heartache!!!
Can love last?
I say hell no!@#%^!

CHANGING HEARTS

I've changed?
How could this be?
I am still the one
Who before you
Would drop to one knee.
I am still the same man
Modest, funny,
And could melt in your hands.
Though the years has gone past
And time has stood still
And love has fled
To the abandoned dark hill
But I still have the same Heart
Full of love and joy
Bouncing around
Like the holiday birthday boy
My Heart never changed
My tears still flow
All of my life
From my inner soul
Lovely lady in dreams of mine
Know this and remember
My love for you
Will always be for all of time.

February 13, 2000

<u>KEEPING IT INSIDE</u>

HeartSender: Asami, what's wrong?

silence

HeartSender: Asami, what's wrong?

silence

HeartSender: I know that something is wrong.

a tear falls

Asami: No, nothing is wrong.

July 5, 1999

<u>ONCE BEFORE</u>

I loved once Before
Or was it twice?
It amazes me how I can recall
The very essence of her beauty.
We were young
And old in dreams.
We were excited
To be free.
Two different paths behind us—
Two different paths ahead of us.
We were never two of a kind.
She always brightened my day
Each moment I laid eyes upon her.
For the life of me
I cannot recall her name
But I can recall how she
Danced among the stars
And swam among
The moon's glimmer.
All in a lifetime
She was made for me.
All I had to do
Was to let her know
That she and I
Were meant to be.
Yes, I fell in love
Once Before,
With a stranger to my arms
Who dazzled me
With her humor
And with the gleam
In her eyes.
I could never replace
The magic she brought to me
Nor will I ever love someone
As much as she made me

Love her
This stranger to my kisses
Is someone I knew so well
This stranger is the one
I loved ONCE BEFORE.

July 13, 1999

BEST FRIEND

One of those treasures
We seldomly find.
A gift of smiles
To ease the mind.

A birth of sunshine
Delivered at dawn.
A shooting star
Celebrated with wine.

A golden emblem
Worn with pride.
Red velvet sheets
With secrets to hide.

A tropical flower
Ecstatic to bloom.
Young inexperienced lovers
Embracing the midnight hour.

With innocent Hearts
To never mend
Nothing is more special
Than my BEST FRIEND.

WHAT KIND OF WOMAN?

Well I see what you like
From the beginning to the end
Of the kind of man
Who will have your Heart to win
But what kind of woman
Do you now claim to be
That this man should devote his love
For all of eternity
Tell me why you now think
That you have what it takes
To enter a love
With out making major mistakes
For I am the HeartSender
Requesting your reply
Awaiting to give you the love
Your Heart will never deny

June 22, 1999

TWIN OF THE BRIDE

Little sister
I bow at your feet
Singing the songs of old St. Al's
Laughing, searching for dire needs
—I look up to thee
Let me go back to the days of tomorrow
To find what we lost
Among old tears
Can you find the lost smiles or broken feet
To see me lurking among your admirers?
I smile for you and all that you are
Telling you that I can not live without you
Not knowing that all is forever
As all is my love
From brother to sister
And sister to brother
I stare into my own eyes
To see you happily sad
Let not the arms of another
Take your love from me
Simply set it on a mantle
To always look to in time of need
I am your twin and equal half
Who will battle the world
To be at your side
From day one I was there
To hold your hand
And even now
To give that hand away
I rejoiced at St. Al's
Among the crowds
I rejoiced at old Shaw
Among the press
I rejoiced among the Gophers
In a well acclaimed spirit
Now I will rejoice here before you

As the one who loves you the most
In time we lasted just past twenty-nine years
Now I pass that modesty
To another.

Heartsender

July 26,1999

PASSING ON

TONIGHT IS FOR THE MEMORIES
I LEAVE TO YOU UNTOLD.
THROUGH TIME AND TIME—
A SAILOR IS PASSING ON.

NO MORE RISING SUN
TO HIDE THE GLIMMERING MOON.
FROM LAND TO LAND—
A SAILOR IS PASSING ON.

ROLLING AWAY FROM ME I CAN SEE
THE DESERT GOLD DANCING FOR ME.

THREE YEARS IN THE MAKING—
FRIENDS SAY FAREWELL.
FROM BROTHER TO BROTHER—
A SAILOR IS PASSING ON.

<u>JUST TAKE ME!</u>

Take me!
Take what I am
A man so strong
With a Heart so weak
Take my body
Do as you will
But leave my Heart
For someone who will love
I walk with you
Knowing you are not true
I sleep with you
Knowing you don't care
So take all of me
Except what I treasure
Leave it!
For true love
Will come find it.

August 23, 1999

NOT MADE FOR LOVE

Not made for love—
A curse of a birth
To walk among those in love
Never to embrace that feeling
A sad toast or gesture
To the passionless ones
To go through life—
   Or should I say following years
Because without love
  There is no life
Just wasted time in years

I was made not to love
Like Romeo—So Heartless
Moving tears through the night.
What star could light my night?

She was made not to love
Like Juliet—So cruel
Dancing rhythmless upon my Heart
What fool can lie at her feet?

We were made not to love
Like Akiko and I - - So impulsive
Spinning the moon around and around
What eyes could turn away from them?

Give Romeo the Heart to love!
End the tears from her eyes
So she can see the star's light.
But I was made not to love.

Give Juliet the passion!
So she can sing a melody
And dance to my tender Heart.
But she was made not to love.

Give Akiko and I patience!
To slow down time
And close all other eyes from our kisses.
But we were made not to love.

August 24, 1999

<u>GOODBYE AKIKO</u>

Goodbye Akiko—
—For now

A short goodbye

How many times in my life
Must I utter that word
   A broken voice
Watery eyes—
   Sadden Heart

Though a short goodbye
   Time is thy enemy
With promises of a speedy hello
My Heart moves slow.
   Counting each beat
Each second
   Each minute, each hour
Each day.

Why can't I stay
   In your arms
And sleep the night away
Why can't we love
Each other for a lifetime
I breathe your essence
And nourish from your smile

Goodbye Akiko
—For now

I must part from
Your warm embrace
And treacherous whisper
That leaves me helpless
   At your feet

Goodbye my love
—Till next I whisper
    My Heart into you

Goodbye

ABOVE THESE CLOUDS

Above these clouds
   I fly in this chariot
Thinking of her
   With lips still warm
From my intimate kiss goodbye.

The pain hits me
   Tomorrow - - Her face
I will not see.
   The day after - - Her smile
Will not brighten my day.

I beg you horseman
   To turn this chariot around!
Let us travel back
   Through the storm clouds
And mass of stars
   To the love of my life.

I give part of her Heart to Joanna
The rest belongs to me
   Above these clouds

Let no other man
   Claim what I have
Learned to need
Let no other lips
   Passionately utter a song
Upon her lips.

Like these clouds
   I am afloat upon
An overwhelming mass of life.
Just last night

I felt her passion
And regret still
    From letting go.

Love is a petty thing
    More than love
Is what I always felt with her.
Even now—
Above these clouds.

September 5, 1999

ONE MORE TRY

One more try
   Pondered through my head
The head of a fool
   A father? A Dad?
Lady Blue
   What will you say to her?
No dinner dress for dancing
   Rents gone Honey!
One more try
   A disease or weakness
I fight without a weapon
   Miles away—the hotel
Taxi fare in hand
   In a strange land.
Go for it!
   You can't lose!
But I have already lost—
   From One More Try.

CHASING HEARTS

Hold now, this moment
In the back of your mind
For the HeartSender
Will forever now pause time
I chase a dream
Far and wild
Ever since these emotions inside
Stop being that of a child
I chase with close thoughts
And let things happen as it may be
For the thrill of the chase
Develops a lost soul's sanity
So run as you have been
Away from what is dear and tender
And hide while you can
From the chase of the HeartSender

September 6, 1999

SHE LOVES ME

She loves me
   This I do know
Her kindled smile
   And blushing eyes
Tell me so.

She loves me
   But dare not reveal
To me or to herself
   As her wave of emotions
Stand still.

She loves me
   Even though it hurts
For I am not a lover
   Yet a man in bondage
Living out his curse.

She loves me
   After all these years
As I counted her smiles
   But being a fool—
Ignored her tears.

She loves me
   And accepts what I am
No secrets or lies
   No kisses nor
No trust of this man.

She loves me
   But in her eyes I see
That I love her
   —Timidly as
She loves me.

September 9, 1999

SHE SLEEPS

She Sleeps
   I stare into her mind
Are her thoughts of me?
   Her hands
Loosely hold my gift—
   A teddy—my prize
Her pillow—a part of me
On this crowded train
I stand before her
   Only her in my world
Should I kiss
   This sleeping beauty
And awaken her from her pose
NO!
This moment is mine
   As only my eyes
Cover her—her blanket
Her hair falls
   Over the arms
That comfort me
I am her prince
   For now—denied her touch
But it is I
Who loves her—
   As she sleeps.

IMPATIENT HEARTS

Hold me my sweet tenderly
I've been waiting impatiently
For you to fulfill my every fantasy
I just know it must be destiny
For us to bond spiritually
You must think I am talking crazily
But I know that you are the one for me
Just let me prove it rightfully
And the light of love you shall finally see
I am a man who is readily
Prepared to love you steadily
And kiss you down carefully
But you must trust me totally
And know that others will only envy
The love we make erotically
The HeartSender I may claim to be
Giving you my love's only key

September 14, 1999

<u>SECRET ADMIRER</u>

Have you ever loved someone
   But knew they didn't care?
Have you ever felt like crying
   But knew you'd get nowhere?

Have you ever looked into their eyes
   And said a little prayer?
Have you ever looked into their Heart
   And wish that you were there?

Have you ever wondered where they are at
   And wondered if they are blue?
Have you ever wondered who they are with
   And if their thoughts are of you?

Have you ever walked up to them
   Then stuttered on what to say?
Have you ever told them how you felt
   Then watched them walk away?

Love is sweet but hurts so much
   The price you pay is high.
If you had a choice between love or death
   I would rather say goodbye.

True love comes then true love goes
   That is how it must be
For love is a priceless gamble-
   A hopeless fantasy.

So don't fall in love my friend
   You will hurt before it's through.
You see my friend, I ought to know
   Because I fell in love with you.

September 19, 1999

<u>WITHOUT A KISS</u>

Trapped!!
Confused!!!
Wondering which way to turn.
Unsavored lips lead me astray.
My mind only thinks of her.
How could this be?
Denied the sweet taste of love's gateway
I find a kingdom of laughter
In a horror house of love
   Forbidden love
The worse kind of love
   Love without a kiss

Without a kiss - I am only yours
   To love faithfully and to hold
A liars way to gain a prize
   As the hurt in his Heart unfolds.

Without a kiss - I am at your beckon call
   To catch and cherish all your tears
The jester's games for the queen
   As he cries for her through the years

Without a kiss - My world stands still
   In need of only you
A sailor's promise to return
   As his lady awaits the time through.

Without a kiss - You are on my mind
   Each passing moment that goes by
A coward's hour to face his fears
   As time releases a slow cry

September 26,1999

IT

Did you see IT?
Did you feel IT?
Did you reach into IT's definition
    And pull out IT's true meaning?
Did you see IT in my eyes?
Did you hear IT in my voice?
Did you feel IT in my arms?

Do you know what IT is?

IT is what wakes a man up.
IT is what puts a man to sleep.
IT places a smile on my face.
When IT is gone -
    IT takes that smile away.
IT makes the warmth run
    Upstream to my Heart.
IT runs wild in the forest
    Of pine trees on a winter's day.
IT makes comets change courses
    And armies sacrificial.
IT keeps me coming back to you
    And you coming back to me.
IT is what I always felt with you.
And what you always felt with me.

<u>SOUTHERN HEARTS</u>

Down south is where I want to be
Between your legs giving you total ecstasy

Taking you places you've never been before
Tasting every drop as you beg for more

Taking my tongue on a never ending trip
As it gives you pure joy between each moist lip

Going deep past that mysterious bit
Tasting those juices, making you submit

Beneath your naval deep in your treasure
It is the HeartSender giving you so much pleasure.

October 3, 1999

<u>LOST IN APRIL</u>

I search for a bitter breeze

My mind spins
   Around and around

A lost touch
   A lost soul
The warmth overcomes me—

   Lost in her love

Her gentle smile
   And gentle sounds
Explodes from all around me
Harsh whispers stir me cold
   Escape is passionless

No gentle kisses
   To guide me away
Caressing every part of me
Lost again and again
   Lost in ecstasy

Winter's gone
   Spring's far away
Summer's hiding
   As the pain exhales

The quicken sweat
   Never dries
As the innocent eyes
   Never lies
My name is called
   Again and again
Pulling me further
   Away and away

My hand
    The left one
Has no mercy
Exploring-
    Awakening-
Every part of her
Lost without hope
    Lost without a promise

My body rebels
    Her every movement
The heat
    Too much
The cold
    Too much
Confusion
    Never existed

Deeper
    Further
Slower
    Faster
No Guidance
    No follower
Lost in her World
    Lost in her love
Lost in reality
    Lost in my imagination
Lost as my life spills away
    Lost all alone

Lost in April

KNOWLEDGE OF LOVE

I knew true love
I am happy to say
And I shall know it again
One bright uplifting day.

FORGIVING HEARTS

Forgive me
Temptation has taken control
I know not what I say
For desire has a hold
Look not at these words
I say unto you
But feel my words
Giving you a love so new

October 6, 1999

<u>CONFUSED LOVE</u>

If I loved her
Would I kiss another?
If she loved me
Would she accept my wondering kisses?
Strange, her emotions
Strange, my confusion.

She looks at me with wild eyes
And I look at her friends with desire.
Is this love?
Is this how love should be?
Strange, her trust
Strange, my confusion.

I walk away when she calls
She answers my letters I never write.
We tend to make love each time we meet.
We rarely find time to meet.
Could she possibly love another?
No! I give her the love she needs.
Strange, her love
Strange, my confusion.

LAIR OF HEARTS

I felt your message
From far away
Telling me, begging me
To forever in your arms,
...Stay
I thought of you
Each day and each night
Enticing you, and luring you
To love me and hold me
...Tight
We thought of love
There in mid-air
Misleading us, and taking us
Into HeartSender`s golden
Lair

February 10, 1999

A LONG WALK ALONE

Stepped off the brow
Looked eastward
A dark gray sky
Hovering over
An almost peaceful blanket
One might call the ocean.

Only darkness

On an endless pier
With land ahead
A ship to my rear
Named home of two years
A destroyer of two hundred men
Searching for world harmony

Give me liberty
Or give me Beer.
Single were some
Married were none
Deprived the good life
Of freedom
A brave sacrifice
A very lonely one

Unforgettable running lights
On a dark gray frame of a sky

Breath away- for now

The walk began
Continued from a week before
No destination

Heartsender

Okinawa
An Island paradise
The warm breeze
And clashing of the taunting waves
Drove thoughts of despair
First love
Second love
Last love
So many lovers
So many Heartbreaks

Searching for a beginning-
To this walk?
To a reason?
To an answer?

A little boy
A corner
Head in arms
Tears in hand

A young man
A world
Life in confusion
Tears in Heart

Each step into this paradise
Leads me further
And further into my own mind

My son, I've never seen
My son, I rarely see
But I sail
And now I walk
I walk alone towards paradise
But for me without love
There is no paradise
Just a long walk alone

FROM THE HEART

No book bares
Such intimate thoughts
No book can harvest
What losing true love
Has taught
For I utter
What most constantly seek
That one emotion
That makes the strongest man
Ever so weak
I am the HeartSender
Living out his curse
Giving others a chance
To avoid what truly hurts.

AMONG THE BLACK WAVES

Lights in the distance
Among the black waves
Some move away
Some stand still
Music
Jamaican original
Warm light breeze
Among the black waves

They call this place
Sint Maarten
They call this place
Saint Martin

The rain trespasses
Upon the night
The music keeps playing
The dancing never stops
On this island
Among the black waves

I listen close
Hearing the palm trees sway
The never crescent moon
Reflects a picture
Among the black waves

Sint Maarten
A treacherous scene
For love
Love from strangers
Never meant for memories

Fabiana she whispers
In her native tongue

Fabiana
I called on
Never to say no
In any language she knows
They say her job
Is for sinners
They say her job
Is for the strong

I try to imagine her
This island girl
Even as she stands before me
I try to forget her
This island girl
Even as I hold her
Sin I am living
Among the black waves

Our lips were not meant to meet
Our Hearts not meant to speak
She held on for a promise
I held on for an answer
Why now?
Why her?
This angel
Among the black waves

<u>INSTINCT OF THE HEART</u>

You say to have control
But I am a man
Strong and bold

I can't hold back
These feelings inside
Knowing it is your lust
You try so desperately to hide

Even now I see upon your right breast
A masterpiece of art
Each of my hands wish to possess

And fondle so with great care
Giving you pleasures
In your sweet cherries lair

It is Instinct that I blame
With thoughts of erotica
That only your love can tame

October 15, 1999

IN THE DISTANCE

In the distance I find myself thinking of you
Your wild long tamed hair and eyes of blue
In the distance I am by your side
To love as each day goes by
In the distance can you hear me call your name
Wanting you, needing you without any shame

Days go by and people may change
This man you once knew has a love that's strange
Close your eyes and feel me come to you
And expand the life and happiness you once knew
Alone your Heart will live again and again
To the power of this whispering mortal man

In the distance you want only me
To let go and hold for all eternity
In the distance there is no other
Who expels any desire you ever felt for another
In the distance we moved as one
Stride by stride into a world so lonesome

Take me away to where you dwell
And make a scene of a lover's fairytale
Young love, old love, people of desire
Heartbreak, lovesick from the burning fire
We fell in love in an instance
And our love grew in the distance.

THE STALKING HEART

Sleep if you can and hopefully fall into a dream, But it will be I standing over you with my favorite ice-cream, I would have brought yours but it will be I doing the licking, spreading it all over as your desires start a kicking. Yes I am hungry to taste each gentle spot, From your left ear lobe to where it's awfully hot. Sure that is not where I will stop but first I must hear you beg, as I rub my tongue up and down each leg. "Come Inside!" you softly, desperately cry, As I answer your plead spreading apart each luscious thigh. Slowly I enter into the depth of your lair, As all of your insides go up in a glorious flare. First slowly then faster, then even faster, taking you further away from your every day disaster, Then slower, then slower, then even slower still, As the tears come pouring against your strong will. Then faster, then faster, then even faster, As you finally know why the HeartSender is the love master.

October 24, 1999

FIRST ROSE

Age of the times
Way back when tears were meant to fall
I dwelled among the happy ones
Or so I wanted to be

Almost free
Just past time of innocence
I lived a wondering journey
Into my own soul
And into my own Heart

Like the glorious ones
Like the happy ones
Like someone else
I wanted to be.

Eyes of mystery
I always solved
Lips of sin
I wanted to commit

Did she know?

In our walk
Secrets were told
In our walk
We fell in love
Or so it seemed

Could I ever see
Could I ever hear
Could I ever feel
That thing called love

Heartsender

To be young was a crime
To never know was a crime
Oh to be free at Heart was a crime

Each step I wanted to make was made
Each step I wanted to take back was lost

Tell me brown angel
Am I hers
Is now the time for me

Lost tears fill my Heart
As she will always be
My first rose.

October 26, 1999

LOVE

So many have tried
So many different ways
So many answers to this question
So many - So many - So many -

In my mind - there is no answer
In my mind - there is no other way
In my mind - I never tried
In my mind - In my mind - In my mind -

Let me take you back
    To where it all began
For in the beginning
    Is where the answer lies

I am a boy - shy and timid
I am a man - weak and strong
I am all that I can be.
So many promises
My Heart never made
So many tears
My eyes never seen

Not looking for it
Was my biggest mistake
Not being prepared for battle
    A war I could not win
    A fight without a defense
    A knight without armor
    A man without a protected Heart

Thief!!!
I cried into the night
Searching for a reason
Searching for an answer
Searching for help

The PAIN!!!
   To the thought this feeling
   May someday depart

I began to nourish
   From what my eyes could not see
   From what my lips could not taste
Crippled to no movement
How could this be?
How could my life be taken?
   Taken into a realm of a different world
   Where the rainbow always shined
     Without the rain
   No darkness, No sadness
How could this be?

The dancing pedals
   The rose once glorified
The swimming melody
   The song once enlivened

With closed eyes
   I've seen heaven
With closed ears
   I've heard her Heart beat

No longer - My time
No longer - My smile
No longer - My world
No longer - My Heart
No longer - No longer - No longer -

It became - Our time
   I didn't squander
It became - Our smile
   I nourished from
It became - Our world
   I spun around
It became - Our Heart
   I cherished
It became - It became - It became -

There was no escape
There was no going back
I had been taken by her glamour
I had been awakened by her gaze
It came into my Heart
   So furtive
It came into my soul
   With beligerence
I wanted to fight
   To send it away
I wanted to fight
   To keep it with me

I am not the same man
   Who laughed at the past prey
I am not the same man
   Who waltzed over other Hearts

Funny - I am not the same man

I carried a rose
   What splendor
Five small pedals
Protected by five larger pedals
Together the fragrance
   Unmatched
Together the beauty
   Unsurpassed

Like love
   The rose lives alone
But love is not the rose
And the rose can never be love
But love went away—
If those feelings
I felt had that name?

I could not think
I could not eat
I could not stop the voices in my head
I could - I could - I could

Heartsender

Pain is all I felt
As my sleep went away
And the nights got longer
And the rain kept coming

I prayed for help
I prayed for an answer
I prayed for the pain to stop
I prayed - I prayed - I prayed -

I know not love but Heartache
That fatal feeling which caused me
To now give up my life to Heartbreak

If I ever felt love
If she ever loved me
If love does exist
If I was meant to love
If - If - If
Then let me love again

October 28, 1999

?

Be careful of what lurks in a wish
A kiss
A tear
A bitter smile

I wished for _____ once
It may have come true.
But in the end
My happiness parted as well

Be careful of what lurks in a wish
Your genie may bring you happiness
   —FOR NOW

UPON GOLDEN WINGS

Upon golden wings
    My love soars with you
Visions upon visions
    We dance
In the mirror
    I see your inner smile
Upon soft clouds
    I feel your love storm forming
Dark angel of laughter
    Come sing with me
The melody
    Of long lived legends
They cry so softly
    For the love we make
They envy from a distance
    As the happy tears fall
Can you feel
    The earth move below us
Can you feel
    The stars coming closer
Can you love me
    Upon golden wings

November 24, 1999

IN CHAMBERS

The room - small, crowded
Four milk cartons - scattered, empty
Six mats - no vacancy
Peach walls - cement floor
On my feet - shower sandals
On my body - orange jumpers

Life of a criminal?
Did I deserve this life?
Forty miles over on an empty bridge.
Not to pass 55 - never crossed my mind

My thoughts are of Asami
My wife to be?
The love of my life?
Have I found love
Or have love found me?
Was I blind in a confused love?
Tomorrow - Would I love her?

Her Heart is Pure
Her love is Pure
My Heart is Black
My love is Black

Oh genie in a bottle
Answer my wish
In between three walls and bars
Let me part with the knowledge of love
This poet, this lover, this sailor
Locked in a chamber far worse
Than what these bars confine him to

Laughter - he hears is not shared
The silence he hears is not seen
My eyes in the middle of the day
Are the only eyes to witness this moment
The moment the Heart is released.

December 09, 1999

A SPECIAL MOMENT

I looked up into a starlit sky and all of me shook. Only her smile took my eyes off the shooting stars. Too old to be shy and too young to leave without getting what I craved. I craved the touch of her lips. I just wanted to let myself go in her arms and never return. I needed this more than she could ever realize. A simple kiss would steal my Heart away and wipe away the many years of loneliness and Heartache I was cursed to live out. She looked at me as if she knew what I wanted but dared not give me notice that she wanted this even more. I pulled her close to me staring deep into her eyes. I am not the one to smile when I have thoughts of desire on the mind. She let her body go and gently flowed in the direction my hands guided her. At this point I knew that her body was under my control and I could do as I wished. But what did I truly want? Did I want to make endless love to her through this night? Our lips were still strangers and the stars were becoming impatient. She broke the ice or should I say that she lost control and forced her lips upon mine forcing me to open up and except her completely. I tasted her sweet embrace and became lost in the moment. I held her tighter and began to explore savagely then gently as time stood still. My hands became great explorers and explored the forbidden parts of her body. Still I needed her even more. I did not want this to end. But before I did something I would regret, I had to bring that special moment to an end.

NEEDFUL HEARTS

The Heart is always
By your needful side
Touching you and loving you
Bringing tears to each eye
Even as the night
Slowly turns into day
The Heart is wanting you
In the most exotic ways
For now is the time
That we are apart
But true love will be sent
Straight from the Heart

21 January 2000

PASSING MOMENTS

Don't break my Heart
As the tear ran down her face
The time untold
As the secrets in her eyes unfold

How could I speak
Or even reply
Holding her then
Wanting her in sin

With flesh on flesh
I was a low life man
Out for pleasure
Tasting her sacred forbidden treasure

I kissed away
Any doubt she had
Knowing that deep down inside
I was taking her for a dead end ride

In the passing moments
She needed me
And I needed her
So intimately

In the passing moments
I froze time
And kept my wife
Out of my mind

In the passing moments
Her body, I pleased
Even though
Her Heart, I teased

Heartsender

January 26, 2000

PRICELESS-

    That was all I could say
    As I watched ____ pass my way
    No diamond could ever take ____ place
    As I sketched a masterpiece of _____ face.

February 4, 2000

IN PASSAGE

The tears kept coming
    To no end
The blame was mine
    Once again

No more promises
    I shall make
Falling in love-
    A big mistake

I try to please her
    The best I can
But over and over her trust
    Abandons this man

To the couch I go
    To find some peace
As the pain in my Heart
    Will faithfully release

I didn't mean
    To make her cry
I guess this relationship
    Is one big lie

The end of this love
    Is almost near
As these walks increase
    Year after year

Oh HeartSender
    Just go to sleep
And awake with a love
    You promised God to keep

February 22, 2000

HOW I LOVE THEE

How I love thee
Upon this starlit night
I shiver to the thought
Of laying thy eyes upon thee

Thou art the sun
Twas lights thy life
Thou art the river of love
Twas flows to thy Heart

Oh how I love thee
Angel of the Rising Sun
For love is all thy need
Oh how I love thee

February 23, 2000

<u>LOST PEDAL</u>

At last thy sent thee down
For love is lost to beckoned crown
Thou art willing to fight
Thou art a coward in flight!

So much beauty I see in thee
So hopeless thine own envy
Dark red feather away
Dark red feather thy prey

Be gone! I command thee now!
In plight oh shameful foul!
Thou must die to Heartbreak
I must live in Heartache

Find thine rose from hence thee spawn
Travel in swift from dust till dawn
Thou hast no need of passion this night
Lost pedal, I have no need to fight

February 23, 2000

<u>HAPPY 30TH</u>

I sit and think of all we had
I sit and think of you
I sit and think of what could have been
I sit and think of what we've been through

I sit and think of our first kiss
I sit and think of our last tears
I sit and think of the happiness we've missed
I sit and think of all those years

I now wonder who is on your mind
I now wonder who has your Heart
I now wonder who will last over time
I now wonder who is keeping us apart

But what happened was meant to be
But what happened was our destiny
But what happened didn't go our way
So I am truly thinking of you
On your 30th birthday

UNCONTROLLABLE HEARTS

Don't control
What comes natural
Listen
Feel
Consume it's pleasures
Don't hold back
Sit back
And enjoy
Each moment
Each utterance
Each breath love gives
Take it and see
Control is of the past
Letting go
Letting my love in

February 25, 2000

<u>INTO OWN EYES</u>

A *broken lamp, scattered pictures, and a half eaten pizza. Torn sheets, dirty laundry, and a table covered in bills. No music, No light, No life. A man stands making faces in the mirror as if he wanted to be someone else. Behold he speaks...*

    What calm sea should you swim?
    At last you have made a mockery of all
    Let alone a mockery of him

    What calm sea should you swim?
    A damsel in distress you claim to save
    Against all morals with a soft whim

He pauses and splashes water on his face to wash away reality, then turns away.

    I am not the one you toil and tame!
    I am not the one you fool
    I am not the one who turns away in shame

    Close thy eyes and open thy Heart
    A black day has come to play
    To set your life and body apart

    He laughs.

    Laugh you will my lonely fool
    For all is forever wrong
    And your love is a useless tool

    The pain has come to stay
    No more silence in her tears

    A soft cry.

You have made her happiness go away

She was not the first to harvest.
So turn and look deeply
Look! Repent! And confess!

He turns to face the mirror once again.

Aye! She was not the first!
But as did all the rest
She satisfied my thirst

An animal, a dog, a man
I preyed upon the weak
And relished all I can

I am not the foul one
Who asked for it
Tempting me until it was done

Silence overcame him as he placed his face in his hands. A frightful laugh broke the silence. His head rose then he stared deep into his own eyes through the mirror…

Oh but you were indeed
That frightful predator
They found in a belonging need

The truth they thought you only spoke
To toil and taunt and caress
Until it was their Heart you broke

Never in their life have they seen
Such kindness, such respect
You cruel, selfish, human being!

"You are my love, my everything"
You whispered to them in bed
As your mind was set with another to sing

A soft tear broke the silence in his feelings.

91

Cry you shall for all of time
Remembering those broken Hearts
As peace your soul shall never find

No true laughter, no true peace
As you see your past lovers
Greatest sorrow hopelessly release

Cherish you must the tear you shed
For lost love and lost promises
You made them unwittingly wed

First Allison then Cathy then Karen
You destroyed to no end
Promising them a Heart they could never win

Save us both from this intolerable pain
End this cursed inhumane life
Then true happiness we both shall gain

He reaches for a knife then holds it to his chest
as the tears came with no end. He speaks…

Is this what you want upon this night
Don't blame me for lost love
You were the one who failed to fight

Each one of them I cherished to no end
Hoping and praying that their happiness
Would forever come again and again

I held Allison as my queen of all time
But she lost my trust remember
And it was Heartache we both did find

And Cathy was my forever soulmate
Who abandoned me when I needed her most
To her parents and destiny's fate

Finally Karen, sweet Island girl
Lost my child to the hope of a better life
Destroying mine and her glamorous world

Into own eyes I plead an honorable goodbye
As we both leave this world
Living and loving one big lie.

The knife sinks into his chest
As life, love, and guilt
Is finally put to rest

STATUE OF LOVE

Not an Adonis. Just your HeartSender. I too watch over you as the night goes by. I see each tear you dream and each smile that was lost. I ponder on your beauty that blinds others. So many times I wanted to no longer be a statue that could not hold you through the passing moments and whisper love into your silent cries. I wanted so much to become flesh and feel the passion you undeniably possess. But I was cursed and could only fantasize of being the one you held tight through the night. I could only watch you turn in your sleep reaching for a touch of another. I could only be the one thing that could be kissed over and over again. Yes I am not the Adonis but I am the HeartSender in the form of your every fantasy.

February 28, 2000

DEEP SECRET

Shhhh!!!
There is something on my mind.
I have found love
But my Heart is running out of time.

Is it love? You ask
Maybe not
But for me
Love is something of the past

Why now? Why her
She doesn't have my Heart
But I have tried true love
And it was hell to finally part.

Not just once or twice
I suffered from Heartbreak
Three glorious times
So I am destined to live in Heartache

Why do I keep her hidden
Away from my world?
To escape from the pain
That would soon unfurl

My first love
I will never tell
For a part of me regrets
The moment love fell

My second love
I so boldly told
Though she has the breath
That feeds my soul

Heartsender

Well, My third love
Funny, she is already aware
And it was the lost of her love
My Heart, My life, My soul
Could not ever again bare.

March 16, 2001

HURTFUL HEARTS

Why do men Hurt women so?
Hmmm, That is a question
Answered so long ago.
I am a man, young and strong
With a Heart that could do no wrong
But I have this awful desire
To touch a pure woman
That will set my soul on fire
I vision her night after night
But meet others, giving up this fight
They fall in love and promise to be true
But my mind is elsewhere
On a new fresh body to pursue
I guess I could be a dog out for one thing
But I also have a Heart
That was once broken and never again will sing
Yes this doggish way started when I was young
When I trusted this one woman
That took my Heart and trust to a plunge
I can't speak for all who has these doggish ways
But I know that if I ever find that dream woman
My trust and love with her will always stay.

<u>LOVE'S BLOSSOM</u>

Hidden in Flowers
I see your smile
Upon the right- a collage
Of that never-ending mile
You wore white
Of a satin pure dress
With hopes that this night
It will be love you finally caress
The flowers bloomed
And the wind came gently by
As I yearned for a touch
Of that gleam in your eye
I wanted to be
The one in plight
That would soon be there
With love this ending Spring night
Platinum was her smile
As the sun daringly shined
Oh how I wanted her
To always be mine

THE REPLY

Dear Honey
I know it's been too long
Since we've kissed
And tormented our Hearts so wrong

I just wanted you to truly know
My thoughts are always of you
Where ever this ship may someday go

I hope our son will be ready for travel
Upon my return
As my naval career begins to unravel

I promise
I will no longer again leave your side
And come home
With deep dark secrets to hide

You are my life, my love
My every thing
You are the reason
My soul now sings

Without you
I would be totally lost
As life and death
Would then have crossed

Promise me
You would love only me
And cherish this love
For all eternity

From day one
I was yours to take
As you saved me
From a cruel Heartbreak

It's funny
How we beat the game
And built a palace,
Love's Hall of Fame

Oh my sweet, sweet _____,
Our love was taboo
From the start
But upon this canvas
We painted a work of art

As this ship sways back and forth
Comes a realization
Of what true love
Is really worth

The thought of you
Keeps me going each day
While I play the role
Of a sailor underway

Please be strong
And wait these months through
And please don't ever forget
Just how much I truly love you.

Thinking of you Always

Your Husband

Dear Mr. Sailor

Thank you,
For serving your country so well
Collecting stories
For history to someday tell

Thank you,
For fighting for our liberty
As you unwantingly
Left behind your family

Thank you,
For oh so many years
Preventing millions
From unwanted tears

We know of all the things
The Navy puts you through
And of each day and night
The difficult tasks you do

We also know
How you hold your family so dear
And would fight the world
Just to be here

We know of your son
Your sweet strong little one
For one day he will be like you
So courageous, so fearsome

In his eyes
We can all truly see
Your love, your smile
Your sensibility

Your handsome son
Gives us a reason to live
And we wish he would give you strength
In God to forgive

We know of your sweet wife
And how she is
The center of your life

We know you see in her
The strength to fight
No matter what sad things
I say to you tonight

Heartsender

Like all things
I must find a place to begin
To let you now know
Her life has come to an end

The cause?
I can't explain
God came calling
And the angels came

Your letter
Was by her side
With a smile and tears
Knowing your love
Will last through the years

Much Regret

Red Cross

<u>PEACEMAKER</u>

I set my ways to change my Heart
I plan my Heart to stop future pain
I dance in circles to travel far
I live the life of fantasy to give me reality
I am the self peacemaker

FORBIDDEN LOVE

I salute you Ma'am.
Subtle
In secrecy
I salute you Ma'am
With eyes wide shut
I see your desire
Don't tell me
This desire
Doesn't exist
I salute you Ma'am
With both my hands
And my Heart
Careful!
Others might see
Just what the thought of you
Means to me
I salute you Ma'am
With this forbidden love
Beyond the boundaries
Of this ship
From enlisted to officer
I salute you Ma'am
Beyond this rank
That I am the only one
To fulfill your desire
Close your eyes
And see me
Making love to you
Open your eyes
And feel the emotions
Run through you.
A twitch of your love muscles
Overtake your sanity
Moisture between your thighs
Calls out for me
I salute you Ma'am
With my forbidden love.

ETERNITY

One light I see tonight
One score I want no more
One Heart I will never part
One smile that runs wild
One tear throughout the year
One kiss to answer my wish
One love sent from above
One time I was not meant to find.

March 10, 2000

IN THE DARK

I see the flashing lights
The dark tears
And golden smiles

Red leather suit
High heels

I see the light smoke
Loud music
And golden tears

Brown eyes, hazel

I see your frozen cry

Feel me wanting you
Feel me needing you
Oh so long
Oh so very long

I see your golden tears

You need me
You want me

I feel your desire

Crowded room

I hear your beating Heart

Feel my eyes
Searching your body down

Feel my thoughts
Making love to you
Through the night

Feel my golden tears

Each tear I cry
Tonight for you
Is a tear to show
That my love is true.

March 12, 2000

A NIGHT IN CROATIA

I fell in love
In a night in Croatia
Among the tempered waves
And stone walls of Asja.

Broken Hearts
And an empty bottle of wine
Kept my desire for her
Lasting for all of time

Sad trees
And happy faces of laughter
Made our kisses and hugs
Memories made for the night after

Alone, in the middle of the crowd,
On the edge of tears
We embraced our love
And held it inside through the years

No more sad trees,
No more tears for me
I found my love, my soul
I found my eternity.

<u>BETRAYAL OF LOVE</u>

Last night I went out with my friends in a romantic town called Menorca, a small island off of Spain. The temperature was hot and the mood was dangerous. The danger was that I was lonely and there were so many beautiful women. I had a few drinks of a little rum and coke, you know my favorite. Well there was this one woman with eyes I could not resist and lips that fell from heaven itself. We danced all night. My friends were partying as well. We kissed so deeply that I got lost in her kiss. But then something happened. Something that I never expected. They began playing slow songs and in this foreign country away from you, they played our song. My Heart just dropped as my body dropped down to one knee. I felt the pain you would have felt knowing what was going through my mind, knowing what I was doing far off in another land. I betrayed our love. Not only did I have desire for another I also acted upon it by kissing her with passion. I could not get you off my mind. I began seeing you everywhere listening to every word I say, questioning every step I make. I never wanted to betray our love. But I did and it hurts so deeply. I only want to go back and erase those moments I held another, but I can't. Even though you are miles and miles away, your love still has a hold on me.

March 16, 2000

RHYTHM OF LIVING

Sagapo I say to you
   This night
Dancing wild
   Among the harbor lights
This etismos
   I cannot part
As now and always
   I give you my Heart
Walking aimlessly
   In Souda Bay
Hoping you will
   Always stay

Sagapo I say to you
   This night
Para poli orea
   Among the harbor lights
A simple glance
   Makes me smile
A delicate touch
   Drives me wild

Sagapo I say to you
   This night
Embracing music
   Among the harbor lights
The setting sun
   Behind your kiss
You are my rhythm of living
   You are my eternal wish

<u>INVITATION TO LOVE</u>

I have imagined you each night down in my arms as I held you tight. Telling you all of my childhood joys and teenage secrets. I imagine you asking me to love you forever as I gracefully accepted. I imagine you and I in a long lasting kiss. You are the one for me. I always knew that and always is like an eternity waiting to be released from dream to reality. Tender One, come away with me into a world that never sleeps yet the dream never dies. A world where walking on the clouds is just as common as walking upon the pulses of a timid Heart as each beat guides you to another awaiting soft beat. Come and love me and find what your inner self and alter ego directs you to. Come and imagine getting lost with the HeartSender.

<u>MORNING WITH THE HEART</u>

I wake up
But my mind is still asleep
Its cold
Its hot
Its warm
I need you
But you're sleeping
Please awake
And give me more
Of what we shared hours before
Just a little
I promise to be gentle
Oh! What am I thinking
Let her sleep
Let her finish her dream
Maybe it is of me
Of the way I kiss her
Of the way I touch her
Of the way we danced as one
All through the night
But I am a man
I have dreams too
But now my dream
Wants to become reality
Right now I want to kiss her
To touch her all over
Look at her!
So tender is her smile
As she sleeps
So much desire
I now have
So much passion
We must now share
Wake her!
But how?
Should I give her
A gentle shake
No!

I have a better idea
But will she be in the mood?
I must put her in the mood
My own special way
I know what she likes
She wouldn't say no
She would only want more
But will I stop there?
No
She knows that I wouldn't
Here goes

There he goes off and away
As she sleeps
His mind wants to play
Kissing her gently
Upon her bare breast
As his kisses heads south
Awaking her desires from its rest
Slowly his tongue
Finds her secret treasure
As her body shakes
From undying pleasure
She awakes from a fantasy
Into a whole new world
Filled with total ecstasy
As she look down
Into his dreaming eyes
She gave a glorious smile
From his early morning surprise
She grabbed his head
And gave rhythm to her hips
Given him more to taste
From her golden spicy lips
He savored each lick
Like a hungry animal would do
Driving her crazy
From a feeling ever so new
Well the rest is a secret
From the diary of the HeartSender
But that morning was special
One they will always remember.

A STARLIT KISS

Last night I snuck out onto the aft part of the ship. We were somewhere out in the middle of the Ocean. I could see the furthest star so clear. The sky was lit by a grouping of stars that formed your face. Your eyes sparkled from the Milky Way. Your lips dazzled from the trail of the moon. All I could see in all of that beauty was you. Only you. I pictured you on that ranch alone thinking of me. Wanting me. I pictured us riding into those rolling hills and into the grass where we will make love upon my return. Those stars kept my sanity as I look up to them and vowed my love for you here in the middle of my piercing soul. I could only rejoice in the passing moments that will lead me back to you. As I could hear the rolling waves all around me attempting to break my concentration on the ways to love you slowly. I became lost in those stars hoping to lift myself and kiss the trail of the moon just once. I promise to hold this moment in my Heart just as long as the stars shall shine. Your HeartSender.

March 17, 2000

BESKRAJNO LJUBAV

My zauvijek zena
My house of ljubav
I look upon the noc
And shed a golden tear
Hvala, Hvala, Hvala
Ti made my zivot free
Ti made my srce sing
Hvala, my zauvijek zena
Ljubav has found ja
Ljubav has stolen the noc
From muskarac to zena
And zena to muskarac
Ti are my zauvijek zena
Ti are my beskrajno ljubav

Heartsender

March 17, 2000

SONGS OF VIOLET

I too heard the violet sing
Among the running breeze
Across a sea of dark blue
The melody I craved
The silence I wept

I too heard the violet sing
In a sunlit harbor
Through sacred walls
The chanting I held
The love we made

November 2, 2000

MYCHAL

A brief stop in a restroom I had
Handing out towels
I met the most inspiring lad

Michael was the name
He most proudly claimed
Who told me to follow my Heart
To reach your fortune and fame

Ironic was the name he bared
For the son I never met
Is named Mychal
Whose love I desperately spared

My Heart is with poetry and family
I now see with open eyes
From the wisdom of a stranger
Whose life is barely getting by

For the son I failed
To relish a fight
I promise to you we will meet
One teenage night.

Ten years has parted
Between you and I
Family love is what
We both shall never again defy

To Michael, the one
Who set my Heart straight
I thank you in secrecy
Upon a drifting Hearts fate

Heartsender

And to all of you out there
Who are not following your Heart
I beg of you to open your eyes
And give a happy destiny
A helpful start.

FOUR OF A KIND

A simple glance
I knew they came a long way
Sharing a table
Traveling where ever
Their Hearts want to lay

One in sweats
Yet posed control of her life
One in a suit
Worn specially for this night

One in jeans
with a cigarette in hand
And one in slacks
Taking her final stand

Oh how the laughter and smiles
Took over the scene
As the memories
And broken glasses completed this team

Eight hands on four different cheeks
Led me to believe
This ritual takes place
Week after week after week

Two hands displayed a diamond ring
As four Hearts
Made life forever sing

VALENTINE'S KISS

From a distance I will be your Valentine
Loving you in ways
That will ease your restless mind

I will love you slow from head to toe
Telling you all the things of love
You would refuse to ever let go

Though I will not be there to look into your eyes
You will think of me
Loving you slowly as this special night goes by

Too far to grant you your intimate wish
As I long to give you
That one special Valentine's kiss

DREAMING HEARTS

Look
Feel
Me making love to you
Touching, caressing, devouring
As I take one hand
Unto your breast
Slowly massaging
Slowly remembering
Your pulse
Your speeding Heart
The pure flesh of warmth
Bringing my manhood
To full strength
Laying you down
Beginning at the left toe
The tongue travels
To each
And every neighbor
Slowly remembering
Your Heart begins to race
Your body begins to shiver
My hands caress your inner thighs
Remembering the warmth
My tongue begins to follow
Tasting the trail to your treasure
Remembering the true flavor
Wanting more
I can feel your moans
Your pleading for no more
I find your pleasure spot
And taste its spices
Over and Over and Over again
As your hips begin to roll to me
Giving me more and more
My tongue goes deeper
As your body becomes weaker
You grab all of me
Inserting into your treasure

Heartsender

Feeling its true strength
Its wonderful arrhythmic motions
Going deeper and deeper
Driving the animal out of you
The stride is broken by your
Multiple release
But the pleasure still comes
In circles and depth
But a loud ringing noise interrupts
As I pull away
Into the shadows of your mind
And you awake
To an empty bed
Wondering, remembering
That one HeartSending Erotic Dream

March 23, 2000

UNANSWERED HEARTBREAK

I gave you my Heart!!!
With closed eyes-
I have seen you throw it away.
I never wanted to leave you
But just didn't know how to stay.

With material things
You were so generous,
As I always received the bill?
You promised not to hurt me
So why do I love you still?

While singing you a song,
From deep inside,
I discovered you were without ears,
Silent from love,
Now you are filling my soul with tears.

You should have told me before
Your love was only a fake
As now I must live the rest of my life
Trying to forget this teenage mistake

ASSURING HEARTS

Tender one, even though some of your days do not go well, you will have me waiting in a fantasy to some day tell, Though the miles seems endlessly apart, I will be waiting for you each night, deep into your own Heart. Every time he brings a soft tear to your eye, Just remember there is someone like me waiting to become your forever kind of guy. You have a beauty that he fails to see; a beauty that I always wanted from my dreams to reality. So keep your head up and reach for the sky, Because the HeartSender will never ever let true love again pass him by.

March 20, 2000

IN DREAMS

Drifting whispers
Through my soul
Counting lost cries
Of days gone old

I am ancient
In body and mind
Of everlasting desire
Lost to dying time

Help me woman,
My birthright mate
Regain what I lost
To destiny and fate

Open my eyes,
Inspire my Heart
Send ecstasy
To this forbidden art

I see the lagoon
So shallow, so cold
I see the stars
As time unfolds

Yesterday has lost
To this promising tomorrow
My happiness has become
Replaced with tears and sorrow

The kings are alone
Without their queen and war
The lips are vanquil
In a deep sleep craving for more

Heartsender

Let me taste
Your cherished love
And prey with honor
Upon the white dove

More hours may past
Through this silent night
As you guide me toward
Your glamorous light

Only in Dreams
Did our bodies meet
Only in Dreams
The Heart was released

March 23, 2000

FEAR

Some fear losing life
As the breath gives way
A promise of tomorrow
Has not been kept

Some fear reaching the clouds
As you soar upward
Away from the cradle
From which you wept

Some fear leaving the norm
As daily routines
And habitual ways
Must now part

Some fear the laughter
And taunting stares
Some fear the unknown
And the aging art

Me, I fear more
Than they can ever perceive
For I've seen horror
That can not be relieved

I've seen the lost
And broken souls
I've seen the hopeless
Standing still and growing old

I've seen lasting smiles
Turn into forever tears
I've seen so much pain
Over the past breaking years

Heartsender

I don't want to know
What they went through
I don't want to end up
So sad and so blue
The lucky ones are those
Who fears only flying
Or change, growing old,
Looking foolish or dying

My fear is one
I must find the cure from above.
Of course like most of you,
My fear is love.

April 3, 2000

HEARTFULL QUESTIONS

Do you still love me? (From my wife to be)
Do you still see in me
What you thought love should be?

Do I still make you smile
And make your Heart dance wild
And hold true happiness for a little while?

Do I still make your head turn?
Do I still give you pleasure to yearn
And make your insides burn?

There was a time long ago
When I knew I had your love to hold
To warm me dearly as time unfolds.

But now I am ever so confused
With a feeling my love has been misused
And my Heart relentlessly abused.

You no longer hold my hand
Nor do you claim that you're my man
Casting me out of your life's plan.

Tell me something here and now
In your Heart does love endow?
If so then tell me when and how?

Tell me with you is there eternity?
Tell me now!!! Before I flee
Do...you...still...love...me?

Heartsender

Do I still love you? (To my wife to be)
How could I not love you
After all the things we've been through?
I love you more than time can tell
Long before my Heart's broken shell
And before the heavens fell

Oh how I still love thee still
I will make you my wife until
The stars fall and life is to kill

So please don't ever doubt
What true love is really about
For I will make your Heart shout

Yes my love I still love you.
Each breath, each Heart, each moon of blue
Makes me know that I still love you.

I love you
    My wife to be!

LOVE AGAIN

I came home from a hard day's work. The first thing that came to my mind was you. I walked in and our dog was asleep. I walked all through and you were no where around. I sat the white roses in a vase disappointed that I could not see your smile that I dreamed of all day. I sat down lost in my now weary thoughts of the ways I wanted to just take you into my arms and make love to you wherever you were. I wanted you in the worst longing way. I felt the desires building up in me I could not hold back. I tried taking a long cold shower but the water bounced off of me boiling. I needed you. There was no cure. There was no turning off this animalistic desire. I got dressed and went on my search for you. I went to the bar that we met. It was a long trip. The beating of my Heart made the time go slow. I walked in and saw you there with the smile I thought of all day. Should I take you there in the middle of this crowd, as they would watch in envy of the love we make. NO! What am I thinking? I turned away and headed out the door. Without knowing that you saw me or maybe you felt my presence. You followed and called out to me but I thought it was my mind playing tricks on me. You then caught up to me and I could feel my pulse raising to an unknown land away from reality. My insides jumped with joy. "Oh how I love you" were the only thoughts on my mind. If the feelings that I feel is not love then damn love and the definition that they gave it. Without a word we spoke for a lifetime in each other's eyes. You knew everything that transpired in the passing moments before. I was nervous as if it was my first time. But we made love before many times. That night we bonded in body and in soul and no ONE will ever tell me…That I…will ever…Love again.

Heartsender

April 2, 2000

<u>FIRST WHISPER</u>

I wanted to tell you I love you
When we first met
And when we first kissed.
I wanted to tell you I love you
Every time
My eyes saw your face.
I wanted to tell you I love you
Every time
I heard your voice
And heard your name
I wanted to tell you I love you
Oh so many times

Thinking of you every day
And every sunset
Thinking of you every night
And every sunrise
Makes me now before you
Want to whisper
I love you every moment
That passes by

Look into my eyes
And feel me wanting you
Look into my Heart
And feel me loving you
Look into my soul
And feel me worship
Your every smile
And your every kiss

I love you! (Soft whisper)

MODELING HEARTS

You are a model posing for me each day
Showing me a desire I had hidden away
But I try to abandon those unrealistic thoughts
From what the lost of dreams has gracefully taught

March 31, 2000

NOT YET

Morning you (facing the mirror)
A beautiful day for a run
At age 16
And my life has just begun
I now have no time for play
And with the young ladies
I now have no time for fun.

Morning you (walking alone)
Football season has past
Prom was last night
Oh the memories we made
In my Heart will always last
No time to settle down
College bound I go
And the parties I heard
Will always be a blast

Morning you (blowing out 21 candles)
Life is perfect as I was told
She is out of my life
And one love I will never again hold
But it was much too soon
To settle down with only one love
Too soon to live the life
Of a man growing old

Morning you (blowing the horn stuck in traffic)
Calm down! You're running a little late
Deadlines past
Hope has been defeated
By time and fate
Oh the horror of last night
Never again will you ever
Go on another blind date

Morning you (A candle light dinner all alone)
Today was your day
The ending of decade number three
So much has happened
So many unsolved fallacies
There is love in my life
Or so I have been told
But not the love I can claim
As the days grow old
I still think back
To the days of yesteryear
When I found love
When I found my golden tear
Am I ready to settle
To end this losing bet
I look into this dying flame
And whisper to myself
NOT YET!

<u>EROTIC CHRISTMAS NIGHT</u>

I opened the door
Then slowly walked in
Wrapped in only a bow
Stood you waiting for love to begin
I could see what you wanted
By the gleam in your eye
For me to give you the loving
That makes your soul cry
I pulled you near
Kissing and caressing you so tender
Adding to your desires
Into your bodies sweet surrender
Oh what a present
Sent from a above
As there in mid-air
We made unforgettable love.
As I laid you down
Still deep inside
You called out my name
As your prince of tides
Over and over and over again
The passion came at no end
Over and over and over again
It was your Heart I claimed to win
Then I saw them fall
Those fresh bitter tears
Letting me know that it was always I
Pleasing you these past beautiful years
An Erotic Christmas night
It came to be
With HeartSender granting you
Your every fantasy.

April 7, 2000

<u>WILD HEARTS</u>

The scene is set on a dark night
   A pair of lovers
     Claiming their destiny's right

With the will to overcome the horror of fate
   Our HEART SENT lovers
     Unleash their desire to mate

But as with all love stories once told
   Tragedy must strike
     As the love in their Hearts unfold

Among the black waves far and away
   One must imagine
     What their own Heart has to say

The swaying of palm trees and handmade fans
   The footprints in sand
     And the clapping of hands

For the first time in Mychal's life,
   The offspring of his father,
     Channing, and he emotionally unite

For twenty years he knew of no dad
   Or birth honored mother-
     Just fairytales gone oh so bad

A gathering of cheerful souls and lonely smiles
   Places us close
     To where these Hearts begin to run wild

MYCHAL:
Oh what a night to live
To experience the magic
That God has to give!

137

CHANNING:
Yes, brother this is true!
This night is filled with magic
And it's all because of you.

Twenty years has passed us by
And now we finally meet
To end my curious cry
I learned to know no one is to blame
Just take life as it comes
And toss your regrets into the dying flame

Here's to our dad who you now know
Sailing the world
Keeping us in Heart and a part of his show

MYCHAL:
All my life I knew of only him by dream
A boy's fantasy
In a childhood lived downstream

Always wondering if he had love for me
To cast me out of his reach
Away from a world I wanted as my reality

You were so lucky to have him close in life
Celebrating holidays and first steps
Though your mother too never became his wife

CHANNING:
Son of a sailor I came to be named
Awaiting holidays and special leaves
Falsely smiling when ever he came

MYCHAL:
Oh to see his face just once a year
Would have engraved on my face an eternal smile
Instead I was forced to clutch to a golden tear

CHANNING:

Oh my brother, think cheerful and don't be misled
Time has taken a lot from us both
But it was our father's tears I've seen shed

He was tired from a battle he knew he could not win
But with the touch of an angel
Your fate I almost shared and his dreams came to an
end

So tonight we drink to the good times to come
We are family through thick blood
And now we will be family with past hardships to
overcome

MYCHAL:

Drink hardy tonight I will
For first drinks are special indeed
For I drink with a renowned Heart to fill

But take heed brother there is danger in the air
It is said that nights like this
Gives any Heart the desire to forever share

And for me and you not ever knowing the touch of a
lady
We must be very careful
For we are targets to land another Heart for all
eternity

CHANNING:

Don't worry brother for I learned from the best
Our father taught me to hold back
And always keep two just in case one fails the test

Tonight I will not fall in love under these lights
No matter how beautiful she may be
Or what magic you believe has control over the nights

Heartsender

Over the mountain yet so close by
  Dancing the forbidden dance
    Wasting years with love under a lie

We interrupt a conversation for two
  Disagreeing on things pretend lovers
    Seem somehow to always do

THIS POEM OF A STORY WAS STOPPED MIDWAY THROUGH
TO RAISE YOUR CURIOSITY OF WHAT THE HEART CAN DO
FORGIVE ME IF THIS ACT SEEMS TO BE CRUEL
BUT SOMETIMES EVEN THE HEART CAN BE OVERRULED
I PROMISE TO FINISH SOMETIME DOWN THE LINE
AND REVEAL HOW WILD HEARTS OVERCOME THE TEST OF TIME

HOME AGAIN

Today, my ship anchored upon the shores of Egypt, in passage through the Suez Canal; deep into the Heart of the Gulf. I stepped out onto the hard sand and thought of you. I wished so much for you to take that step with me. For the first time I was home again in a place I'd never seen before. I thought of all the pain of past memories of loved ones I never knew. I thought of the voyages they took into closed arms of agony. A tear dropped from each red blistering eye as I tried to search back into the secrets the rolling sands keep. But I seek comfort in the memory of you holding me that last intimate night. I seek comfort in your distant smile and wind traveling whispers that I can still hear over the thundering cries of yesterday's tears. I was home again in a strange land as I searched for your kiss through the dense clouds. I was home again in the memory of you.

April 10, 2000

NEEDFUL THOUGHTS

Flowers need sunshine and water
To bloom
All I need is your love
With the sun and the moon

I need your smile
To get me through the day
As I look into my own Heart
And stumble on what to say

I need your touch
And passion through the night
To fulfill my desires
I have for you under the heaven's light

I need your voice
When I am far away
To sooth my spirits
Thinking of the years beside me you will lay

I need so much of you
It hurts down deep in my soul
That I know that I will always need you
As this body and Heart grows old

SONG FROM THE HEART

Funny how I could vision you there on that stage. It was as if you were there singing to me. I could see those tears fall from your eyes hoping that you could see the tears I cry inside. "Love me forever Nomadic Heart, Give me My dream before you part, Life's a poetic circle coming from within, As our love shall never ever end, Love me forever Nomadic Heart, give our love a peaceful start." I sat back in the shadow listening to each word of this song. But could not respond because I was far far away. I wanted to be there only for you. I wanted to be the melody that came from your lips. I was that Nomadic Heart you sung of. I was the fire that burned inside of you. I was all that you wanted but I was away, loving you, kissing you, being the flame you could not put out. The nights grew long as I still sailed away, I could still see you up there on that stage. As the crowd came to their feet They applauded for our love. They yearned for that feeling as well. They wanted what you held inside. They want to be apart of that ring of everlasting joy. They wanted our love.

April 10, 2000

WANTING MORE

Is it wrong of me to want a little more
Than the few words
And little gestures you have given me before?

Giving a little more will not hurt you
For I have given you all
And all is what you should give too!

A little more will make my tears go away
As each day I wait…
And each day I go down on one knee to pray

That you will look deep down inside
And find that little something
You try desperately to hide

A little more!!! I know you can
For I have seen it in you
Before you sent it away to a far away land

Friend of mine for all of time
Give me what I need times four
Give me just a little bit more.

BACK TO THE LAIR OF HEARTS

I drifted once again into a world that you ruled—my dreams. I could get lost in this world and never want to find a way out. There I am walking over water and through fire across the tainted landscape of my desire. I arrived to a place that took my breath away. I arrived to a place called the Lair of Hearts. In the Lair of Hearts is where we will make love. I saw you just walking through the knee-high grass dancing to the melody from my Heart. I approached you slowly contemplating on how to kiss you down after this long awaited meeting. With each step towards you the ground shook from the beating of my Heart and quickening of my pulse. I could hear your smile and feel your whispers. I was becoming a part of you before I ventured inside of you. I was becoming lost in this new land. But I must stop this fantasizing because it is self-torture. Being away from you only forces me to get lost in my dreams. I just wish you were here tender one.

WEEKLY PLAN

Okay honey, I have been thinking.
I feel that something is missing
And I am to blame
That our love life is sinking

So I came up with a simple plan
To put that fire back
Where it is meant to be
And give you all of the loving
That you can possibly stand.

On Mondays I will start it off right
With aromatherapy
And a full body massage
Giving you pleasure throughout the night

On Tuesdays in the evening after eight
The clothes will come off
And desert will be served
As I feast on you till the bed breaks

On Wednesdays I will slow it down
With a midnight walk through the park
Attempting to seduce you
Under the moon's jealous frown

On Thursdays there will be a big surprise
As I read you poetry in bed
And being the man that I am
Simply hold you tight until sunrise.

On Fridays I will take you out
Showing you off
As the woman who stole my Heart
And makes my soul shout

On Saturdays the decision is yours to make.
You can go out with your friends
Or you can be home with me
As I wash your hair and bathe your body
Giving you all the loving you can take

On Sundays, what can I say?
The end of the week has come
And all Hearts will wish they were ours
As they vision us where we lay.

<u>TONIGHT I DREAM</u>

Two months has gone by
I am not yet half way there.
So lonesome the journey
To reach you once again
So tonight I escape
Escape to a world
Where only you lie
Tonight I dream
That I am with you
Telling you all I've seen
These past six months
Telling you of
The palace ruins of Croatia
Telling you of
The Harbor lights of Souda Bay
Telling you of
   The rolling waters of the Suez Canal
Telling you of
   The Sand storms of Bahrain
Telling you of
   The gold souq of Dubai
Telling you of
   The diamond mines of Israel
Telling you of
   Country streets of France

Tonight I dream
That I am making love to you
Throughout the night
As if it was the first time

REPLACEMENT OF THE HEART

Tender one, It is not for my honesty that you should still love me but it is my love for you that you know will never go away. If I was alone with her I don't know what I would do. Would I wish that she were you? Yes! Yes! I wish that on every face that I see clouded by the tears in my eyes. I wish you were here each passing moment I breathe and each step my Heart takes in a beat. I wish for you upon each wave that flows towards me. Oh how I want you to be on one of those waves flowing past the starlit sky into my arms. It hurts. It hurts so much.

<u>POWERFUL HEARTS</u>

Powerful,
Fulfilling
Are my thrusts
Your nails
Dig deep
Your teeth are clinched
As deeper and deeper
I thrust at no end
Thinking of you
Taking you
I pull away
As your juices run wild
Looking into your eyes
I can see you wanting more
I turn away
And begin to depart
But being the man I am
I return to finish my art
I lift you in mid-air
Placing your thighs
On each shoulder
Sending my tongue
Deep into your treasure
You placed your hands
On the ceiling above
Begging for an end
And begging for me
Once more
I toiled in your juices
Standing proud and tall
As your thighs squeezed my head
And your body shook once more
I then laid you down
On your hands and knees
Placed an low arch in your back
Then entered from behind
Deeper and Deeper
And deeper I went

I grabbed both your hands
Your shoulders touched down
Still deeper and deeper
And deeper I went
Faster and faster and faster
The sound of flesh clapping
The sound of air releasing
The sound of juices spraying
HeartSender, HeartSender,
HeartSender.
I heard over and over and over
AGAIN.

SWEET FLOWERS

Sweet flowers
Blooming to the sound of making love
A rose of no color
A lily
This flower bed I make with you
Is nourished for all eternity
I do make love
So sweet
Upon your sweet surrender
I too feel the over pulse
Of two Hearts joining

Close your eyes
And vision only I
As I come to you
Prepared to love you down
Feel my hands searching
Every part of your body
Feel my eyes
Reaching deep into yours
Seeing your desire
Seeing your want for what I have to give

The candles of Croatia
Burning the light into our souls
Of Jasmine
Of Lavender
Of the oils I rub into total pleasure
Painting a forever climax
Into your memory
And we make love
So soothing
So smooth
So slow
So gentle
So deep
So rhythmic
Bringing all emotions

Out from the layer
From which they slept
Every Heart which loved
Could feel our love
Every pair of lips which kissed
Could taste the sweet sweat
Pouring down our face unto our lips
Yes we kissed and died over and over
And over again
Not wanting to live with out dying again

Sweet flowers
Scented to pause time
Sweet flowers
Blooming as we make love

FAITHFUL

I tend to look into my own self.
Love stricken?
Confused yet no longer curious?
Will my Heart last?
Only time can tell?
Not true!!
Only my Heart can tell!!
Deep down inside I know its real.
Love has taken away all doubt.
I am near that threshold
Where love gives immortality.
Yes!! I will be immortal.
I do.
I do?
I do!
I DO!!!!
It is in my head and will stay.
Soon it will be my reality
And my Heart will finally be claimed.
Tomorrow I will see her eyes.
Tomorrow I will feel her Heartbeat.
Tomorrow I will be her soulmate.
Tomorrow I will be the man
She wants me to be.
But will she still love me
For the rest of my life?
I know this to be true
That these lips will not wander.
This Heart will never go astray.
This man will only love one.
This man will be only hers
For the rest of my days.
This man will forever be
Faithful.

April 25, 2000

CRESCENT MOON

A fool you made me out to be
Promising me love and happiness
Before you flee

Never again will I look up to you
For guidance and assurance
As I search these final days through

And to think that you never failed me before
Until now just when I needed you the most
As you left my Heart alone on the shore

April 26,2000

FLASH FLOOD

I call on you
    Treasure among the sands
To take away her unbridled gift
    I carry from land to land

Promise me
No more raining tears
Will turn to gold
    Through my dying years

The fool was I
    To trust her kiss
As even now
    It is her embrace I miss

Hatta is where
    I will sit and wait
To fall at your feet
    And face my fate

I am captured
    In your natural springs
Thinking of all the ways
    She made my Heart sing

Treasure among the sands
    Come to me now
And release this sorrow
    I have at hand

April 25, 2000

Will You Marry Me?

Will you marry me?
And all the little things
Which make me Me!
Will you accept who I am?
So simple yet so complex.
I have my faults
Some are simple
Like wearing two watches
Or being a billiards freak.
Some are so complex
Like money mismanagement
Or lack of exercise.
Yet these things
Make me Me!

So will you marry me?
And show me to your family.
Will you tell them that I am
A sailor with a son
Who will devote his life with you
Til' his final day is done?
Will you tell them
That I am not of their nationality
That my religion is undecided
Yet that I love
With the Heart of an Angel?
Will you be proud to face
Any disagreement
They may have of me
And know deep down inside
My love is where you want to be.

Heartsender

This road I ask of you
Is not an easy one to pursue
For there are obstacles
That even I fear
Should I had to be the one
To choose.

So beautiful lady
I am now down on one knee
Asking you a simple question
With all of my Heart and last breath.
Will You Marry Me?

April 29, 2000

<u>THE FALLACY OF LOVE</u>

A drifter among us has come to play
To learn of that thing most want
Until their dying days

Like all nomads who travel the lands
What this drifter encounters
Is a mirage among the endless sands

Dubai he whispers into his own soul
That love will not come to pass
From legends grown old

But surely a legend must someday come true
Just as his Heart searches
For that paradise for two

Abandon all notions that are branded on the mind
Of love and all the wonders
It promises to give over time

Our drifter has found what really lurks in the air
Yet from his treacherous experience
Our own Hearts have been spared

So sit back and relax as the answer comes from above
And share with me a story
Of a Heart going through the fallacy of love

SORRY I GUESS I DID IT AGAIN
DID NOT FINISH A STORY
THAT HAD YOUR HEART TO WIN
FORGIVE ME PLEASE, I DIDN'T KNOW
WHAT I WAS THINKING OF
BUT YOU MAY ALREADY KNOW ABOUT
THE FALLACY OF LOVE

A DEFEATED HEART

I admit defeat to your tender eyes
I admit defeat to your luscious thighs
I admit defeat as your smile appears
I admit defeat with joyful tears
I admit defeat to your beauties surrender
I admit defeat as your HeartSender

DREAM SERIES DREAM#1

Soft whispers in the wind
The curtains flowed upon moonlight
A swift surge of desire
All is not so
All is not for my eyes
I feel her touch
So distant
So enticing
I feel her kiss
So deep
So wet
Footsteps led me astray
Footsteps in the sand
I entered the darkness of her lair
I entered upon her kingdom
So many voices
So much confusion
Turn away!
Leave this cursed place!!
But I could not
I would not
I needed the pleasures
This place promised
I needed to feel her forbidden treasure
I stepped further towards the massive realm
Sprinkles of moans I shivered
Closer and closer
Reaching and reaching
Still no touch
Still no pleasure
Still no kiss
I screamed for a taste of her
I screamed for one sample
Begging like a beggar
Hunting for my prey
In this jungle of lust
I was not the lion
I was not the hunter

Heartsender

I soon became the prey
Her hands found me
Her kisses dazzled me
Too much!
Too much pleasure!
Too much of her
I needed to escape
I needed to get away
Away before there was no escape
Her tongue found my tender ear
Her lips found my beckoned neck
Her hands found my hardened chest
Her nails found my enslaved back
Her treasure found the depth of my manhood
I was hers for now
I became hers for all of time
I became lost in a world she ruled
I became lost in my own dream

IF YOU LOVE HIM

If you love him
Tell him
Tell him all the reasons why.
Don't wait too long
To let love pass you by
And let him slip away
Seize the moment
And make his love stay

If you love him
To him make it clear
That all in a lifetime
It will be your love
That will always be there

If you love him
Before him, drop to one knee
And ask for his hand of love
Before he forever flee

If you love him
Don't keep it hidden
Let him see
Just how hard
Your love can be driven

If you love him
It is now time to confess
Just how long
You adored him
Above all the rest

If you love him
Forever remember this
That love comes only once
Even without a kiss

April 23, 2000

MY ASAMI

I sit and think about her
My Asami
My wife
The first night long ago
In a bar in Sendai
I looked deep into her eyes
And I knew
She will one day
Have all of me
And I will have all
Of her
My Asami
My wife
Each night we were together
Is fresh in my mind
In the first year
Our love was new
In the second year
Our love grew
In the third year
Our love took us
To a place we both knew
A place lovers worship
And broken Hearts
Search for freedom
My Asami
My wife
All in a lifetime
She was made for me
All in a lifetime
I was made to keep
A smile on her face
My Asami
My wife
My lifelong love
My lifelong friend

ANATA GA HOSHI

Shooshoo omachi-kudasai
Otomo-sasete-itadakimasu
Sabishii-desu
Okimachi-wa yoku wakarimasu
Omaneki-itadaite arigatoo-gozaimasu
Watashi-wa Homer-to mooshi-masu.
Hajimemashite, doozo yoroshiku

DANCING HEARTS

Two steps toward her
I hear her Heartbeats
Two steps away
I hear my desire
Come to me upon this night
Come and don't withhold
The spinning lights
The dancing
My mind only wants her
My sanity has left
Crazy thoughts of love
Here!
In the middle of the dance
But we can't
We must not
We should not
We kiss
I can feel all eyes on us
For a moment
The eyes have left
Or so I make believe
Her lips gently touch my neck
My chest-now bare
My hands begin to explore
Past her silky blouse
Past her linen skirt
Stop!!
Take control!
Not here
She taunts me for more
She feels my manhood
So strong
Full strength
I taste her neck
Her body jumps
Giving me more
More of her grinds
Oh where is my sanity!!

The dancing lights grow dim
She releases my manhood
Unseen to others
Please stop!
Please go on!
They believe we are dancing
They believe wrong
She takes me
So deep
So cruel
Deep into her treasure
My body jumps
With pleasure
With ecstasy
She rolls and dances
As we kiss
We kiss away all eyes
We kiss away the dancing lights
There in the middle of piercing eyes
I found joy
So erotic
So enticing
But am I sane
Grow up!!!
Go find a room!
The stride is wild
The music stops
But we are still dancing
Still deep within her
Still kissing with passion
So moist is her treasure
Unforgettable
As I held her tight
With all of my strength
I tried to withhold
The passion
The noises
But they knew
They also knew why
They envied us
As there we gave it our all
Binding together

Heartsender

In our own little world
Among all the chaos
We could sense their jealousy
But no longer cared
As she led me deeper
And deeper
Into her treasure
Then finally
Yes! Finally
We both shook
We shook of relief
And ecstasy
From our own little dance.

MOMENTS AWAY

I open the e-mail
Anticipating her reply
A beggar of love
From the distant cry
Soft words upward soars
Lifting me higher and higher
As my Heart yearns for more

Who would have thought
On the lonely streets
In a far away land
That little old me
Would find a voice of peace
Away from the vale of no dance

Over the Red Sea
Past the horizon
We exchange our thoughts
Again and again
Bringing our lives
A little bit away from the end

As the time grows
A promise to meet
Stays on my mind
That the creator of my smile
Would appear at the end
Of this long dark mile

But to my surprise
As I drop down to one knee to pray
That the thoughts of
The love of my life
Is just Moments away.

ENCASED HEART

That was deep and unrefined.
To save the encased Heart
From the lost Hearts of time
Was it I who captured your pain
And found in you
What true lovers rarely gain
Tell me tender one from your tender lips
Was It I who took your world
On an unending pleasure trip?

LIFETIME FRIEND

Not long ago we met
Not long ago we shared tears
Not long ago we parted

Over the years I thought of you
A brief call to say hello
A share of laughter
A show of care

Though attempts have failed
To join again
You always knew I cared
You always knew my love was there

And now my needs have come again
But to protect the Heart
I must let you know that you
Will always be my lifetime friend

PLEADING TO FREEDOM

Today I found my Heart astray
Attempting to love again
Has failed to no dismay
It is funny how You try and try
Just to find out all over again
That true love is simply a lie.
Over and Over again
I try to tell myself
That this is all a bad dream
But reality sinks in
And reminds me in a cruel way
That my love life is meant
To sink somewhere down stream.
I ask you love god of the North
To bring back my love!!!!
I beg of thee come Forth!!!
I must regain the strength
In my Heart to live once again
I must get back that love I lost
As these feathers soar with the wind.
To all of you who loved before
Take heed of what I now say
Look deep into your own lost Heart
And swear that you will love no more!!
I am just a peasant in this kingdom
Of the lost souls
I am just a king to all the fools
Of wishes grown old.

CUORE ITALIANO

Shhh! Let me tell you
Meo amore
Something troubles me!!
A night in Trieste
Bello donna Italiana
Bello donna Italiana
Is all I could say
All in a night my life
Has forever changed
I know, I know!
I know!!!
Soon we will be married
But in a moment
I was cursed with
Cuore Italiana
A simple glance
Changed me
As she walked towards me
A simple crave
Tore me apart
As she passed by
Your face was forgotten
Your love was silenced
The endless nights
We made passionate love
Would have been sacrificed
For one night
No!
For one hour
No!
For one moment of embrace
One moment for eterntia
Eterntia, eterntia
Forgive me
Meo Amore
Meo Amore
Her eyes
I can't forget

Heartsender

Her smile
Replaces yours
My desire is
Only for a love
I can never have!!!!

RUM AND COKE

Italiano
A simple drink
Back in the day
A hug
A kiss
A simple embrace
From you
Passes through my mind
Another sip!
My mind begins
To recall
Our last kiss
Back seat
No!
At your door.
I never want to let go
More coke please!
Denied a soft buzz
More rum!!!
Please slow down
My hands
Begin to explore
My lips upon your thighs
My Heart in your control
Stop the drinks
Stop the memories
Stop my love
A moment in Italy
Three tables
Five chairs
Five sailors
And all I think of
Is making love to you.
Curse you!
Curse this damn drink!!!
Curse my Heart!

Heartsender

Let me just pass away
Into this drink
Into these memories
Into this night
Into my own Heart!!!!!

June 6, 2000

EROTICA

Pure lust
Is all I feel
Curse everyone
Who feels the same
I walk around pretending
I walk around with a smile
They all do the same
Out here in the middle
Of nowhere to live
I know that I am not
The Only Lust Walker
I know that I am not
The only one who craves

She walks around pretending
That my eyes don't follow
She walks around with a smile
Knowing that it is I who has lust
Who has the desire to break her
The desire to fulfill her every wish
Curse her as she pretends
A simple touch of her lips
A simple thrash of a whip
A simple thrust!!!!
I dare not think that again
Self-torture are these thoughts
Self-torture are these cravings
Maria, Maria, Maria
Oh how I crave your touch
Oh how I need your loving
Your unspoken healer
Of every sin I have ever forsaken
Begotten walker
I need only you for the moment
Tomorrow
I may not remember you

But Oh today
Today I am yours
And only yours
A walk around a circle
A trot around the world
A clash of the titans of love
So many wonders to unleash upon you
So many kisses
So many encounters
So many of a lifetime
I have this lust
This desire
But others do also experience erotica
Erotica, Erotica, Erotica
So plainly clear
So distant the truth could be
A slow walk around this circle of life
A slow walk around this desire
No!
This lust
This animalistic craving
That only she can satisfy!
How trapped I feel
How weak I can be
Just stop!
Just stop time and memories!
Just stop this Heart of ecstasy
To feel her skin
Her soft rosey plush skin
Beneath me
Beneath my gaze
Beneath the heavens
As our sweat mixes
Sending a scent of love through the air

I know this to be true
I know that I am not alone
I know that others do
I know that others deny
I know that lust walks among us
In every step
In every cry
In every laugh
In every song
In every boundary of Erotica

EYES OF ENTRAPMENT

I hear the song
At first whisper
I hear the melody
So soft and dear
Like a wolf
I prey unto the flesh
Wanting
Needing
Begging for a taste
Would it come freely?
Must I use force?
Force of nature
To force the desire
Built up
Teased
Caressed
A simple glance
Began this horror
Deep into her eyes
Deep into the boundaries of hell
For heaven would not torture me
For heaven would not tease me
Eyes of valor
Eyes of innocence
Eyes of desire
Eyes of my ending
Would I have
What the eyes promises?
Would I taste
What her body has to give?
Eyes of Entrapment
I dare not give into
I dare not stare
I dare not let her power
Overtake me
But just a taste
Just a moment of her flesh
Just a sample of her treasure

Oh what light lies beyond
Her fountain of ecstasy
Oh what dawn breaks
Into this lonely night
Give haste to the slow minded
Give haste to the weak
Which is I!!!
I am the weak
I am the lesser fool
Who stares into her eyes
Knowing the danger
Knowing the desire I will feel
Knowing the fantasies
She promises
Eyes of desire
Eyes of lust
Eyes of my weakness
Eyes of Entrapment
I give into you!!!

<u>STEADY AS SHE GOES</u>

One soft-pillaged
One hard-gifted
Together they flow
With the wind
Together they chase
Into their own dreams
In the Navy
I hear the ship's cry
In the Navy
I feel the ship's pain
Upon the heat
Left out to roast
Upon the wind
Battling the waves
In the Navy
I am the ship's dream
In the Navy
I am "Her"
And "She" is I
Two ships side by side
Chasing its mother
To feed
Two ships scorning whales
Amidst the heat
And tainted waves
In the Navy
I hear the ships' laughter
Deep within it's own beauty
In the Navy
I feel the ships' love
Upon each tear they cry
Even as now they part
Two separate courses
And the wind begins
To thrash their bows
I want to be the ship
And each ship wants to be me.

CONFESSION

Even in sleep
My thoughts of you
Run ever so deep.

HOW BEAUTIFUL AM I?

How beautiful am I?
Let me count the ways

My beauty runs far and deep
Beyond the boundaries of reality
Beyond the distant cries
Beyond the unknown stars

So much beauty have I
So much splendor

My beauty runs far
As the rolling hills
And tempered waves
Upon a glorified quake
Some may disagree
Some may beauty hate
Vanity and conceit
I shall not confess

My beauty has life
And breath untold
As no other being
Comes from my most desired mold

How beautiful am I?
For a moment
Close your eyes
And see me above the clouds
As a whisper from my voice
Takes your Heart by surprise

I wake up each day
With a smile on my face
Rejoicing at my beauty
As I face the mirror

How beautiful am I?

June 20, 2000

<u>WITHHELD</u>

A lesser man I have been
As the feelings stayed hidden
While you sat near me.
Ten years apart in age
I kept telling myself
Unprofessional!
But damn!
I'm human!!!
I am a man!
Craving you each moment of the day
Craving you even more when you were near
I just gazed into my own dreams
As you silently spoke
Hoping, wishing, and praying
That it will be I
To be next in your arms
Why!!!
Why didn't I utter
The very ecstasy from my soul
And make you hear
The whispers of love
Deep below the heavens
And above the begging Hearts
It torments!
But I didn't let you know!!
I didn't hint a kiss of desire
Nor did I ask for a taste of your treasure
Lovely lady,
My Heart is waiting,
No! My desire is waiting
No friendship awaits you
No laughter
No hesitation
No second chances
No looking back in regret
The moment came

Heartsender

The moment was there
But eyes were everywhere
Eyes not of approval
Eyes behind the darkness
Teased me
Enticed me
Pleaded for action
Yes, I had my chance
But only for a moment
Only for the time that has departed
As night fell upon that craving
I knew it would never be satisfied
So all of those feelings of desire
All of those dreams of passionate love
All of those yearnings for a taste
All of those momentary needs of satisfaction
All of those wants to thrash my love upon you
Were simply and regrettably
Deniably
Withheld!!!!

TEMPTATIONS

Maria
I dreamed of you last night
Just the same
Night after night!

How cruel you are
In my sleeping mind
To love me and caress me
Slowly and gently
Time after time

Temptations are with me
In hand a flower
Even now as I sleep
Wanting you, needing you
Hour after hour

<u>MALLORCA</u>

Palma De Mallorca
I sat on the side
Of Magalluf
Strange the feelings
Each moment we kissed
Surrounded by history
British in whole
Our Hearts sang
In the spirit of Old Spain
Close your eyes
As we kiss
And see my love in whole
A few drinks
A few kisses
Each time I close my eyes
And encumber my feelings
Past the sunlit beaches
And tanning nude bodies
Of Magalluf
A distant cry
From Palma De Mallorca
The holiday of British
The solidity of Old Spain

DREAM SERIES DREAM #2

How now I want thee
Golden lady upon this crest
That thou would choose me
Above all the rest

I dealt upon thy love
An undefeatable hand
And thou shall challenge all
Across this dreary land

For thou art all love can be
Twas love that thy fear
In season's dreams
Upon the time thou shall be near

I beggeth thee
To take thine Heart
And cast away thy sins
That sets thou soul apart

For desire comes
Upon this evil night
To shed dire blood of ecstasy
Upon thou treasure in flight

Behold a kiss
Comes in great speed
To challenge thou strength
In haste of thy needs

A kiss shall torment
Even in sleep
And change life itself
As bodies begin to weep

Heartsender

A step upon thy throne
As knights do as knights do
And the Heart of a dragon
Let not this desire be true

A valiant touch upon thy breast
I gently subdue
A glorious triumph of haste
Brings tender moans anew

As sleep cries
For thy ending dream
Love battles
For life and teriny

I dream of love
As love's thy only fear
I dream of desire
And shed thy only tear

A LOVE NOT FORGOTTEN

Funny, the letter
Fresh on the mind
A sister's soft caring words
Of a family's most memorable time

I sit with teary eyes
Of the many voices of laughter
From the ones I truly love
Through many times happily ever after

Six lovely sisters
Still by my nomadic Heart's side
Fill me with everlasting joy
Across this world's treacherous tides

The offsprings they conceived
Brings this reunion a special bond
Though my absence brought regret
A revelation of forgotten love would transpond

To Jeannette, Annette,
Tierita, Angela (YaYa), Marnita,
And my twin Holly,
Much love sails for you from this kin
As he claims a love not forgotten

<u>LUV ME</u>

Come and Luv me
With your whispering stares
Come and Luv me
If your soul should dare
Come and Luv me
Beyond this mortal form
Come and Luv me
In this life's gentle storm

DREAM SERIES DREAM #3

Just moments ago my eyes did close
   Strangely among the shadows
      Appears a body in a seducing pose

The face I see is one I do know
   Of a kinder and quieter portrait
      To be a masterpiece grown old

Ahhh the wonders I shall proclaim
   To play with this body
      Along with her Heart to tame

In the middle of this most glorious night
   Comes a passion crossed a deux
      Relishing destiny's given right

Come glory, come screams, and come tears
   Come embracing, come moans,
      And come no more lonely years

NO TITLE

I think this was the first
No I think this was the last
I think this was almost first
Or maybe it was almost last

But what ever the time
It swept me away
What ever the time
It left my soul astray

I think I will never try again
I think I will never go that far
I think I will never come that close
I think I will never ever again trust

Maybe it was for the best
Maybe it was just a test
Maybe it was meant for another
Maybe I should be with another

I think it was meant to never be
I think I was meant for sorrow
I think it was meant to pass me by
I think for me there is no tomorrow

UNREHEARSED VOWS

Only one empty seat far in the back
    As all eyes caressed
        The moment of silence before the attack

His Heart throbbing to a beat of no end
    Reaching for words
        Only his Heart could ever begin

For lovers grow as time passes by,
    Tears begin to flow-
        More than mere love could ever satisfy

The peace is broken by those golden tears
    As each lonely soul
        Witness true love in memory for all of their
        dying years

        Dream Giver, I now give you my life
        Each dying moment
        I shall be your husband
        And you shall be my wife.

        Who would have ever known of such joy
        As I look into your teary eyes
        And swear on my soul
        In giving you my Heart to forever employ

        I am not just asking for a one night stand
        I am on my aching knees
        Begging you for your eternal love
        As I willingly give you my gracious hand

        Look into my Heart and know why I cry
        Look into our future
        As time will pass us slowly by

Heartsender

For love has its own time portal
Just submit to true love
And deny thy Heart is mortal

Look at each wondering pair of eyes
As they envy you and I

Look at each hour we shared
And how we both to Heartache
Were deservingly spared

So I am asking you...
No! I am begging you to become my wife
As each tear I cry tonight for you
Is a tear to show that my love is true.

FULFILLMENT

For once I loved a gentle soul
With kinder thoughts
And kinder dreams
But now I shall evade from love

Deep down inside
I want not love
But peace of mind
Stop foolish thoughts
Stop chasing dreams
Let not the cry of soft whispers
Toil with your need for fulfillment

<u>WILL LOVE BE THERE?</u>

Half a year dear Heart has gone by!!
Missed memories and lost kisses
Floods my vision in each closing eye

I knew what love was before I went away
But all the long letters and short calls
Can't ensure me that, in your Heart, love did stay

Now my dizzy soul is down to only one more week
Until I will have the answer to this question
Denying me the undesirable Heartache my Heart seeks.

Once named love, I can't lead you into despair
For all the world's a playground
For lovers who chose no longer to ever again care

Bitter songs overwhelms these final days with laughter
Of duets we performed hopelessly together
In search of that final smile we both were once after

Again and again I remind myself that it is you I truly
love
Knowing that my world will soon come tumbling down
From the floating rose with no hand landing from above

So I ask myself truly into the love we both did share
Upon my long awaited return into your craving arms
Will...love...be...there?

TENDER KISS

Forget the kiss
That formed your Heart
And branded your soul

Forget the kiss
From your first love
From teenage years

Forget the kiss
From strange eyes
Among the midnight hour
And dancing lights

Remember only my kiss
The tender kiss
That will last for eternity.

DANGEROUS SMILE

Forgive me as I confess
About a love
Whose Heart I shall never possess

A Heart so true
I dare not upon intrude
For lovers will do as lovers do

It is not her eyes-
Luring and graceful
It is not her pose-
Erotic and enticing
It is not the ring upon her finger-
Dedicated and committed
I dare not ignore
It is her smile
Her dangerous smile
I kneel before
It is her smile
So tender and cautious
That belongs to only one
It is her smile
Already claimed
As I wish to become the possessor
Or the one responsible
It is her smile
Her dangerous smile
I live for.

THE POET (ENDING)

"Don't look into my Heart,
For the Heart is a masterpiece
Not to be sold
You may gather your fortune
And bargain at will
To find what you've purchased
Are tears grown old."

Those were the final words heard that night, as he faded away into the moon's light. No one knew why he left but they all knew why he came. So tempered were his movements through each individual Heart. Not a single sailor was left untouched by his magic. Not a single sailor will ever forget as well. Through the Desert Gold, he taught them how easy it was to mend the Heart even in places thought to be of little hope. The Poet he became to be called and forever in their thoughts he shall remain. As the sun set and will surely rise again he promised to return. You can bet there will be someone else ready to see Desert Gold's last dance, as the tempered waves will call for him once again.

A DESIRING HEART

No!
I am not the gentle one
With you
I am
What I am
An animal in need
A man wanting you
Night after night
Day after day
Moment after moment
I desire
I need
I want
The depth
Of your lair
Of your treasure
To go deep
And Deep
And even DEEPER
Over and Over
And Over again
For I am a Lover
With love
I am the HeartSender

WITHOUT FEAR

You say you love me
This I do know
But it is your fear and mistrust
That tends to always show

Young lady hear me
As time passes us by
That love, in my eyes
Should never make you cry

I have been abandoned
By youth and petty games
So if you want my love
Try to put others love to shame

In the distance
Feel what my love has to give
And just once in your life
Open your Heart and try to live

I offer a life
Full of no tears,
Trust, love, and happiness
That will last through the years

From the moment we met
I knew you were to be mine
But you constantly test my love
Time after time

I am asking you now
To bring your Heart near
And love me and trust me
Without fear

BLACK AND PROUD

I knew the answer to your every wish
When I read your page
For the bottom of your Heart
Is where my love takes the stage
The Lord made me black
For reasons that aren`t known
As I too search for answers
That I can call my own
I am black and beautiful
With a body that is strong
I am tender and marvelous
With a Heart that can do no wrong
I love my eyes, lips,
And the complexion of my skin
I love my strength, weaknesses,
And the emotions I keep within
There is no other like me
With skin of a pure raven
There is no other near me
To satisfy that deep craving
I crave of love and answers
That my Heart shall render
I crave of another
To hold the HeartSender

February 28, 2000

HARSH REALITY

Each day most of us are with the harsh reality of situations that do not go our way. My situation deals with the Heart. Everyone has the harsh reality of a broken Heart or a love that they can never have or never have again. Well the harsh reality of my Heart is the reality that I can never have a love that would make my life complete. This love is forbidden love between best friends. You see my best friend is a woman who brightens my day every time I speak to her or receive an e-mail with only one line. Strange, but it is true. Sure she knows the way I feel yet never confronts those feelings. She never tells me whether or not those feelings are mutual or never even crossed her mind. We tend to go through the years knowing everything about each other that some marriages never reveal. I believe at one point in our relationship we spent so much time together rumors were going around that we were intimate. That made us both laugh but it also put a thought in my mind that it wasn't a bad idea. Our friendship survived college tragedies, real world awakenings, and worldly separations. I still make her laugh across the globe and she still puts a smile on my face where ever she may go. We both have serious relationships now and serious responsibilities that we devote our lives to. I just can't stop wondering what it would be like to wake up next to someone every night who makes me laugh even at the toughest hills in my life and who will coach me through it neglecting my immature ways. The harsh reality is that we were not made for each other. We were only made to be friends and nothing more. So now I am on my way to get married to someone I love very much. But some place in the back of my mind I know when the preacher ask me "Do I take _____ to be my loyal Wife to love faithfully till death do you part?" who's name will I want him to place in that blank?

<u>A PIECE OF THE HEART</u>

HITTING THE G-SPOT RIGHT
LEAVING YOU WANTING MORE
FROM THE HEART ALL NIGHT

HAZELEYES

I once fell in love
With a woman.
Her eyes were Hazel
Deep
Alluring
They could mold
The greatest masterpiece
And hold
Your soul
Caressing
Loving
Bringing you in deeper
Into her world
Yes her eyes
Were deep hazel
But they were eyes
I never seen.

WHAT KIND OF WOMAN II

Well I see the kind of woman
You now claim to be
But would you live out
My dreams and every fantasy
You see, I dream of love
Of everlasting joy
The kind of feelings
Any Heart desires to employ
And my fantasies, Well
They are off running wild
Giving them their own deep,
Sensual, and erotic style
This Heart is one
That is so hard to please
Because it is cautious
Of women who would only tease
For what I have to give,
Simply close each glaring eye
And vision these words
Loving you as the night goes slowly by

WANTING TO PLEASE

Tender one
I see that pleasing you
Will be ever so difficult to do
But I am a strong minded man
Who will see that task through
But first you must open your mind
And let the HeartSender give the love
Your Heart constantly desires to find

UNKNOWING HEART

I don't know her
I don't hear her
I don't taste her tender lips
All I know are her tender words
Drifting into my Heart
All I know of this midnight mistress
Is that I need her

CONFESSING HEART

I tried to be nice
But no more
I tried to be gentle
And love you
Just a little bit more
But now I must
Truly confess
That it has always been you
Above all the rest
I am your slave
At your every call
I give you my soul
Just take it all
I can't hold back
These feelings inside,
I tried to hide the emotions
I tried desperately to deny
But you have won
My gracious hand
Now I will give you my love
More than you can ever stand.

FAITHFUL HEART

I am thinking of holding
Caressing you
All through the night
I am thinking of telling you
My deepest fears
And how I will never
Give up this fight
To win your trust
And gracious hand
To be that one and only
Forever kind of man
I think of so much
That I dare not now say
For I am a patient soul
Awaiting that one special day
That you and I
Would finally meet
As your HeartSender
Helps your emotions faithfully
Release

FOOLISH HEART

If I was to drop to one knee
Slowly
Thinking of only you
Will you casually say yes?
But foolish thoughts
For this foolish man
Foolish desires
To have you for a lifetime
I sometimes wonder
If love is real
Or the pain that broken Hearts endure
Is all I will know as reality
Foolish thoughts
Foolish dreams
Foolish Heart

UNCONTROLLABLE HEART

Forgive me
Temptation has taken control
I know not what I say
For desire has a hold
Look not at these words
I say unto you
But feel my words
Giving you a love so new

BEDTIME

Sleep well my princess
Close each eye with care
And know that I await you
In a secret love affair

ANOTHER VALENTINE'S DAY

Valentine's Day!
Damn!
Here it comes again
Taunting me
Teasing me
Of the love
I don't have
Another lonely night
Another missed kiss
But I have your picture
So tender are your hands
Your smile
And the depth of your eyes
It caresses me
It soothes me
Tomorrow is that day
Most lovers
Will be making passionate love
They will confess their love
Just one day of the year
But with you
Ohhh! With you
I will confess it
Again and Again
Each day my eyes vision you
Each time my thoughts
Dream of you
Each time my Heart
Beats for you
There will be no end
To the need for your love
I will nourish
From your touch
I will be Eveready
For making love
To you and only you
I will breathe your scent
And no one
Could ever tell me
That love does not exist

216

It exist in your walk
In your soft words
And in you glare
I can feel you now
Though you are far away
It is happening again
The walking fantasy
Of you and of me
I am in your arms
Kissing you
Loving you
As time stands still
Letting our love flow
As my hands begin to wander
To each part of you
Pleasing you to the touch
Bringing out your desire
Your ecstasy
Preparing you for me
As you begin to sweat
From the heat of my body
As you want me now
This Valentine's Night
But I must stop
It is hurting me
To dream such thoughts
To want you in such ways
That brings me to my knees
But I do know
That if you
Were here
With me
This Valentine's Night
I would satisfy you
Physically in every way
And emotionally down deep
And you will never
Want another
Because this man
To you now surrenders
As your one and only
HeartSender

I ASKED HER.........

I asked her
To hold me
Through the night
To never let go
To dream of only me

I asked her
To look deep inside
And feel me
Feel all of me
Wanting her
Needing her

I asked her
To imagine
A love so pure
The dolphin's gaze
The puppet's stare
Were the only open windows
To the lost souls

I asked her
To let go
Of all the pain
The Collection of tears
The Unwanted memories
And the lost kisses
We never shared

I asked her
To run away with me
To a far away land
Escaping the chaos
Of the big city
And the horror
Of loneliness

I asked her

To simply
Undeniably
Eternally
Unforgettably
LOVE ME!!!

And.........
she.........
said........
        no.

AN UNDERSTANDING HEART

Ahhh! But you see
I understand
Your pain
Your tears
Your laughter
I understand
Your sleepless nights
Yearning
For a touch
For a kiss
For the whispering of those gentle words
I do understand
And I do know how
To give you this
And oh so
So
So much more

WANTING TO KNOW

Pretty as it may be
You still have no love for me
I don't know what to do
To prove that these feelings are true
Woman with eyes I never seen
Explain what love to you truly means

IF YOU ONLY KNEW

Oh how I wish I could
Make each dream come true
Somehow, someway I would

Oh if I could only see
Those hazel eyes
From dream to reality

Time stands still
As we remain apart
Against our will

Oh if you only truly knew
Just how much the HeartSender
Wants to make love with you.

LOVE MAKING—A CHRISTMAS WISH

Dear Santa,
Send me my Queen tonight
To love and cherish
Under the stars gleaming light

Let me kiss her forbidden treasure
And caress each breast
Giving her undying pleasure

I shall massage her inner thighs
With the warmth of my tongue
Creating tears in her piercing eyes

I shall lift her into mid-air
Going deeper and deeper
Into her treasure's lair

I promise to not bring it to an end
Until the sweat of our bodies
Is cooled by Summer's wind

I will tend to each toe with care
Tongue massaging them
To a point her soul can never bare

Santa I promise to do my very best
As my strong body will be hers
Man to woman, chest to chest

SNOW AND LOVE

Making love in the snow
Is what I truly want to do
Each passing moment
As I think only of you

You may laugh
Or shed a golden tear
But know this my sweet
Pleasure will be your fear

For I will enlighten you
Through out this snowy night
And make you beg me
To always hold your body tight

I am the HeartSender
In true form
Showing you His love ways
In this passing winter storm.

A SIMPLE WISH

To taste her lips
I beg of you fair genie
To kiss her through the night
I plead on bended knee
Her deep treasure
I yearn to taste
Her long awaited pleasure
I will one day satisfy
Her soft plush breast
I shall kiss over and over
And over again
I will tend to her every desire
I will tend to her every need
Among the night walkers
And among the night whisperers
Give me her love
And I shall never ask for more

<u>MONDAY MORNING WITH THE HEART</u>

A long weekend I never wanted to end But it is
Monday morning And the work week begins The alarm
clock goes off aloud As I awake to your smile As my
desires run wild But I must not act or even think To
have your body and ecstasy To erotically sip or drink!
I want to begin this week With a timely impressionable
start But I can't get the thought of making love Out
of my desperate weak Heart Get out of Bed! I softly
cry But my hands begins to explore The soft tender
feel of your right thigh Stop this nonsense! You're
going to be late! As my tongue taste each breast
Plotting on you as my eternal mate. You awake and know
what is on my mind As you spread your legs Wanting
what your hands search to find I climb on top
preparing to come inside As you whisper my name And
open yourself wide But I must not speak or even tell
Of the love that was made As the heavens fell But I
was late with a smile on my face And will do it again
Without regret in this life's race.

ANACOSTIA

Anacostia, into my soul A place unknown Where only lovers go Among the winter's warm breeze She came into view Dropping this strong man to his knees Just a kiss from her tender lips Stirred my insides With a heavenly sent gift As I stared into her dangerous eyes I could see her emotions Softly and nervously collide Even as she revealed those quiet tears I knew that I will make her mine For all the endless unspoken years Anacostia, into you I surrender As I will always and forever be Her one and only HeartSender

<u>MARCH ON LOVE</u>

Almost April
Into your eyes
This month I shall give
One unforgettable birthday surprise
The first for me
To spend this day with you
As I promise to re-enact
The lovemaking that lovers do
Though your trust in me
May be far away
I can feel your need for me
Beyond the things you say
Hazel eyes
It is you that I need
On your birthday
Answering your every erotic fantasy

HEART TEASER

Oooh! So you are at work with me on your mind, wishing I was there giving you a little bump and grind, but I have a secret that I wish to tell, I am under your desk between your legs giving your body hell. Don't move just try to concentrate, as my tongue teases your thighs for memories to create. I am a bad boy ready to taste your treasure, As you anticipate the Heart giving you unending pleasure.

IT IS THE HEART

Be careful tender one, the Heart heard your plead,
now you shall feel the wrath, of a man of desire in
need, I won't hold back the power of my kiss, and it
shall be your tender spots, I will fail to miss, It
has been too long since I held another body tight, so
I promise you this, It will be one long erotic earthly
night, so watch your door as the handle slowly turns,
and know that it is the HeartSender, causing your
insides to lustfully burn.

WHAT THE HEART WANTS

I tell you ladies Straight from the Heart
What a strong Black Man desires
From his queen to give his Love a start
He needs her trust and endless smile
To make it through the day
As he works off each desolate mile
He needs her thoughts and gracious hand
Giving him all the love
His soul could ever withstand
He needs her support and casual kiss
Lifting him past life's trials
Answering his desire's longing wish
Finally, He needs her sexual healing so tender
Through out each and every night
As I am your one and only HeartSender.

SELFISH HEART

Well the Heart is selfish. He wants to be the one who takes you there over and over and over again. He wants to be the one with your nails deep in his back as you cry out his name to a melody unforgiven. The Heart wants to be the one in a glorious stride inside of your treasure bringing all his emotions out from the hidden deep roots of his soul. Yes the Heart is very selfish and he wants to be the only one loving you all through the night.

JUST MOMENTS AGO

It hasn't been so long for me
Just moments ago I touched you
Oh so softly
I caressed you slowly deep inside
And heard you tell me
That I was your forever kind of guy
Yes, you didn't know
It was just moments ago
As I kissed each now warm thigh
And whispered a new world
Among the desires you try to deny
Just moments ago I held you tight
As you begged me to never leave
On this Hot Winters Night
Just moments ago I sung in your treasure
And brought the temptress of passion
To yell the howls of pleasure
Just moments ago we were in one stride
And it was I who fell in love
With the wildness you hide

THE HEART KNOWS

The Heart knows of you tender one. He knows of your search amongst all the chaos. He knows that many are in search of your love but you are only in search of one Heart. He knows of the constant irritation of all those men asking and begging for a taste of your love. But he also knows what you seek and what you need in your life. Though the Heart is amazed at the Beauty you possess physically he is more amazed at the beauty you hold inside. The eyes never lie and the Heart knows all.

GORGEOUSDOLL

A picture of three
All gorgeous
All of a human doll
The first, She poses
In black lace
That put a look of desire
Upon my innocent face
There she stood
Revealing a partial breast
That awoke my inner fire
From its long peaceful rest
The second, She sits
In a black button down dress
Making the bad boy in me
Give up sadly and confess
Showing the temptation
Of each light caramel thigh
Breaking me down to my knees
In a foul childish cry
And the third, She pranced
In all wicked black
Taunting me helplessly
To give up this useless attack
Walking towards me
Telling me to surrender
And be her only man
Her one true HeartSender.

THIS I WILL DO

I would first kiss your tender lips
Granting you your most wanted pleasure
Then I would touch you sensually
From your head to your glorified treasure
I would love you like never before
As time shall slowly past
As you would always yearn for more.

<u>HER DESIRE</u>

Awake!
I say unto you
You slept too long
This starlit life through
It is time for you to begin
Being the desire she held within
Awake to thy equal, you dying pretender
And feel the wrath of the HeartSender

KNOW THIS

Tender Lady, because I am the HeartSender
And it will be your love that shall surrender
I am the one who will love you right
Giving you pleasures all through the night
And when I say pleasure, it is not only physically
Yet I will be all over you mentally
You would not be able to get me out of your mind
Because you will know my love for all of time
Yes I am sure of the love we will make
Because I am the HeartSender making your desires
finally awake

COWARDLY HEART

It is difficult to say what I would do. Because at times my shyness makes me out to be a coward. But oh my thoughts are so bold. I would be thinking to grab you into my arms and kiss a whisper of love into you. I would dine in your beauty and lavish every part of you in my eternal memory. I would want to love there where ever we would meet. But I am a coward and may not grab you into my arms and do as my Heart truly desires.

I WROTE FOR HER

I wrote for her
And only her
Deep
Erotic
Unexplainable
Her eyes
I've never seen
Her lips
I've never kissed
Yet I visioned every part
Every curve
Every sensitive spot
I wrote for her
I wrote of the love we will make
I wrote of the emotions we will share
I wrote of all the times
She will call out my name
It was so clear
It was imaginative
It was so true
I wrote for her
As I
Wanted to love her.

SEXY IN DC

Sexy in DC
Is what she rightfully
Claimed to me to be
I see her poetic smile
Binding to me physically
But her eyes
Her eyes
Her whispering eyes
Born on this day of love
A love child
Into a woman
Sexy in DC.

WHAT TO DO?

What do I do with someone as beautiful as you?
Do I sit and stare into your golden eyes?
Or do I ponder at a dream come true as the night goes
slowly by?

PUBLISH ME PLEASE

Well I am trying to publish, Yet I run into so many walls, Desperately reaching for that golden opportunity, As my dwindling weak faith falls, Maybe this year will be my promised chance, That I can make all the lonely Hearts, Standup and give an unforgettable last dance.

STRAIGHT FROM THE HEART

Must I stare into the emptiness you bare, Or shall I ponder in the desire we both share, I try to avoid the simplicity love gives, And dine night after night in the dreams we live, Come to me and close each blind eye, And see the earthshaking ecstasy that time has passed by, I am yet a vision you see each lonely night, Asking for a moment to hold your Heart ever so tight, I am the HeartSender- the only one of his kind, Coming to you straight massaging your tense waking mind.

CALLING ON THE HEART

Some say that sweetness starts from within, that is where my search with you shall begin, I shall first caress and massage your mind, and let your emotions and feelings slowly unwind, taking you on mind trips far and away, as you beg your HeartSender to forever stay, though I know that you are no longer a child, I shall take you to the love nest of the free and wild, just whisper my name and I shall come, to fulfill your dreams as we join as one.

FOREVER YOUR HEARTSENDER

Sweet lady, I thought about your tender words, and was lost in a dream that was once deferred, so easily a man can follow his dark side, and forget about the beauty a woman has inside, of course I am a man as you may know, who has wanted true love in this big final show, I tend to overlook the little things, women express to make their Heart sing, but I am human and make mistakes, seeking forgiveness as his Heart finally awakes, In you I seek what I am truly living for, that one bit of life to make my soul sore, I do have physical needs but they are on hold, to learn more of the beauty you internally hold, so I banish the one you call a pretender, And give you forever your HeartSender.

YOU

If only you knew
My thoughts
My desires
How I crave
For a touch of your essence
Time will stand still
As I listen to your smile
As I hear your gentle touch
As I feel your soft words
I close my eyes and it is you
It always has been
It always will be
You

HYPNOTIZED

Her Eyes!
Her Eyes!
I tried to look away
I tried to be strong
She has me!!
Her Eyes!
Her hair dangled
Upon her right cheek
As she knelt
A seductive pose
The gray hair piece
Only magnified its strength
Yes! I am weak
Hypnotized!!!
Again and again
Her lips I desire a taste
Her warmth I yearned in secrecy
But oh her eyes
Damn her Eyes
I have been hypnotized
I have been captured
I have been tortured
I have been loved
By her Eyes!

THE HEART'S NAME

Sweet one I await to tell you my name
Knowing that it will be your love
I will finally claim.
First I shall whisper it to you
In the most loving way
Then you shall scream it out loud
As you max and beg me to always stay
You want the HeartSender's true title
I sense it in you deep down inside
But know this tender lady
The Heart will have nothing to hide.

<u>EROTIC ONE</u>

Well Erotic One you have captured my eye
Tell me. Do you have room for a sensual guy.
I first want to be your close true friend
But then later I want all of you from the beginning to
the end.

DESERVING HEARTS

You deserve happiness
My little Princess
You deserve to be showered with love
From head to toe
You deserve much more
Than what you received
You deserve a good man
That will fulfill all of your needs
You deserve candlelight dinners
And midnight massages
You deserve to be spoiled
Each day of the week
You deserve someone special
Who listens to your every word
You deserve to be humored
And seduced in just the right way
You deserve to be touched
In every sensitive spot
You deserve so much
That it is killing me inside
And as your HeartSender
I should be the one to provide.

<u>WANTING TO KNOW</u>

Now you say
That I am
That I will always be
Happiness
Ecstasy
Tell me, creative one
Are you the one
I've been searching for
From time to time
Through Hearts and souls
Tell me!
Could it be you.

TEARS AWAY

Please don't Cry
I promise to be true
And do with you all the things
That lovers do

Just look deep into my eyes
And bring your soul to realize
That I am a man true in Heart
Setting your tears and laughter apart

Can't you feel
That my love is near
Yet it is your sadness
I dreadfully fear

What can I do
To take your pain away
And let you know
That you shall find love this day

Tears away
I now plead
As your HeartSender
Is here to fulfill your every need.

<u>A GIFTED ART</u>

The mere thought of you
Coming to me
Inspires not only love
But absence of sanity
For no sane man
Can truly bare
Not having you near
To love and care
I won't lie
To win your Heart
But tell you the truth
Of your gifted art
You inspire me
In so many different ways
I am down on one knee
Begging you to forever in my Heart
STAY

YOUR KIND OF MAN

I am the HeartSender with much love
Being the kind of man you were thinking of.
Just give me a chance to love you down
And make your world spin around and around.

TEASER

Damn, you talk a good game, I must now say, but can you follow your words, and let the Heart come and play, I might let you ride into the night, but it will be you who sleeps first, as I hold you tenderly and tight, You say that you will leave once I fall asleep, but I must be honest, It will be my love you will yearn to forever keep.

Y-ASK-Y

Y-ask-Y
When you know how I feel
Each time you pass by
And my emotions are revealed

Why ask Why
When I dance upon a thought
Of touching and caressing
The love you once brought

Y-ask-Y
When my whispers can't be heard
As I cry out for the passion
My weak Heart deserves

Why ask Why
When the windows of my soul
Releases the pure rain
My emotions can't control

Y-ask-Y
When the love we did share
Was my only
Unforgettable care

So that is Why
I love you still
And will keep that love
Against this foolish will

<u>SLEEP AWAY</u>

Abandoned by sleep
From thoughts of you
Making love to me
The whole night through

With each gentle touch
From your breast to my chest
Led my mind in circles
Desiring your sweet caress

As the lights grew dim
And your thighs became wet
I found a great need
To taste you without regret

Sleep I yearned
To let me escape in a dream
As more thoughts of you
Giving me your erotic cream

As I entered slowly
Into your tender moist lair
I found myself dying
From the fruit it bares

Deeper and deeper
I constantly went
Clutching to that emotion
That was heaven sent

The stars came falling
At the stroke of midnight
As you kept me inside
Holding me ever so tight

That is where
My mind now stays
Making love to you
Keeping my sleep away

UNTIL DAWN

On a rainy, cloudy night
When only your love can satisfy my appetite
I place you on top
Slowly
Feeling every part of you
Gingerly
And as you ride
Into the depth of my desire
I could feel your moisture
Building
Becoming apart of me
You whisper, "Take me!
My black strong Knight"
As you roll around in circles
Feeling the strength of my manhood
As I held your body in midair ever so tight
Until Dawn,
I did not know love
Could be so free
Could be so deep and controlling
Until Dawn
I walked in the blind
Unable to see
Just what happiness could really be
Until Dawn,
We made love
Over and Over and Over again
Faster and faster and even faster
As your treasure throbbed
Through out the night
Each time I took a taste from your pearly southern
lips
You slowly exhaled
With sighs of relief
From the pleasures of this Black Knight
What do you have that drives me wild
Until Dawn?
I need more of you

I need everything you have to offer
I need your tender kiss
I need your tongue slowly caressing
And teasing my ear
I need your hands sculpting my chest
Down to the edges of my love giver
I need you now
I need so much of you
Until Dawn

THE PERSON YOU HIDE

I sit back amongst the silence
I see you
Just as clear
And as beautiful as can be.
I laugh and rejoice
You are mine
And I can be free
Free to love
Free to see in you
What you don`t even see
Even the whispers
You try to hide
Are so clear to my Heart
The stolen emotions
The stolen tears
The stolen thoughts
Are all mine
Are all I need
To be free
The stolen independence you claim
The stolen craziness you hide
The alter ego you caress
Are all apart of you
You!
You! The one I yearn for
Night after night
As I lie back
Upon my pillow top mattress
Looking up at the ceiling fan
Staring at the empty walls
That begs for your portrait
And glamorous scent,
I feel you
I feel your tender skin
Against mine
I feel your precious lips
Upon mine
I feel your piercing eyes

Looking into mine
I feel you
And all you possess
Controlling me
Calming me
Loving me
Night after Night
Hour after Hour
Moment after passing moment
You steal my Heart
You steal my desire
You steal all that I am
As your one and only
HeartSender

<u>BETRAYAL OF THE HEART</u>

Wasted time!
Damn!
What a fool am I
To have love you so
You promised me! Not him!

I should have been the one
Holding you each night
You promised me
Your eternal love!
Seven years I gave you
Seven long years
Night after night
The love we constantly made
Gone!
Given to another
Another man
You are now his wife
You should have been mine
You should have been my queen
I loved you
I love you now
I will always love you!
Those were our walks
Those were our dreams
Those were our everything!
Betrayed,
Disgusted,
Hurtful thoughts my Heart can't bare
No more calls to you late at night
No more dreaming of our future
I am now the fool
I am now the one you betrayed
But I will always love you
Even with this betrayed Heart

A DEPARTING HEART

Oh why must I depart. We have just three hours left before I must meet the fleet. I know you must be weary of the thought of me leaving but it is I who doesn't want to depart. It is I who will be thinking of you each passing moment. I don't know if or when I will return. That is what hurts the most. It hurts knowing that you will be all alone reaching for me in the middle of the night just like you always did and I will be reaching for you, pretending, making love constantly. Pretending your lips are upon mine. Pretending that I was inside of you. Damn, why must I be a sailor. Damn, why must I be so patriotic. Even though it will be my blood that may spill and my nights free from rest, the pain comes knowing that you will hurt as well. That you will have sorrow like never before anticipating my return. In these few hours we have left I will make love to you like never before. I will give you my all. We shall sail away upon the sweat we both make. Off into the setting sun of our future sorrow. We shall ponder in the juices we both make over and over and over again. My Sindra, You shall feel the power of my thrust and know that it awaits you upon my return. I shall place a forever taste upon my lips of your treasure and know of its flavor in the wee hours of the night off at sea. I shall memorize each curve of your breast down past your thighs. I shall make you cry out my name so that I can hear the echo far, far and away. You shall know that the HeartSender will always be with you and you should know that his love was only made for you.

WITH CLOSED EYES

I know that it has been awhile
Since I made your Heart
Joyfully smile
But all I could ever admit to do
Was to always and forever
Think only of you
Time and time you crossed my mind
With hopes that it will be your lips
I one day destined to find
So come away with me
And open your eyes
To your souls fantasy
Your HeartSender

A VALENTINE NIGHT

Its morning again
You're not here
The pain I feel
The desire I see
I walk through the House
And see you all around
Your mark has left
An eternal essence
My Sweet Valentine
My Sweet lady
Tonight will be ours
Tonight we shall make love
Tonight is the night
I will be yours
And you will be forever mine
My Sweet Valentine
My Sweet lady
I continue to seek you out
From the towel that dried you
From the sheets that held you
From these arms that caressed you
From these lips that kissed you down
In every sensual spot
In every tender curve
My Sweet Valentine
My Sweet lady
Hurry home from work
Hurry home into these arms
Hurry back to your HeartSender
Who needs and desires
Every morsel
Every ingredient
Every meaning
Of your love
My Sweet Valentine

REMEMBRANCE OF LOVE

Sindra. It is late. I don't know where I am and I don't care. I only want to be alone with my thoughts of you someplace adrift in this small world. I can remember standing at that window looking out into the tiny lights just off the balcony wishing that this night will never end. A reflection of you lying down added to the beautiful feelings stirring inside of me. She is mine. All mine and fast asleep dreaming of me and the love we just made. I reached for your reflection just to touch a part of you and the wind outside danced upon the glass trying to cool the touch of your vision. My mind drifted again and this time a little further back to that first night we danced. I can still feel your body next to mine and your head on my shoulder with eyes closed as we danced into the stars. I was lost in a simple dance skating on the unseen clouds and wishing that this lady who tore a hole into my soul would never let me go. Would never let this dance end as I held you tight and as you gave into each soft promising kiss upon your neck. I was captured and will always admit defeat to your hypnotizing eyes and knee weakening smile. It's funny how those memories of you are so visual even out at sea, even after the months you have been away from my arms and away from my deep kisses. I must be insane to have gone on this voyage and you must have been strong for letting me leave and waiting for my return. As these waves play a soft melody entertaining my eyes I think of you and all that we share. I think of giving Shakera that Japanese doll I promised her and Devon that Australian Boomerang he always wanted. Just to see their smiles again will bring joy to my Heart As well. Hearing your voice the other day Stirred a feeling in me I could never deny. The softness of each word you spoke awakened that desire you and only you can ever please. I miss you Sindra with ever part of my Heart and every depth of my soul. I reach for your touch even when I am sleeping. Think of me when ever you reach for love. Your HeartSender.

WHERE THE HEART IS

I could not want more than what I have with you. I step out again into the daylight hours feeling the eastern wind over the bow hoping that it was carrying your essence and scent back to me fulfilling my daily wish. As dolphins race along side attempting to be the first to catch the wind I search for, I feel the freedom they share. The freedom to love and go anywhere that love will take them. How I want to be in that school of dolphins leading the way back to your love. The heat of the sun nor the clashing waves would dare hold me back. I take a deep breath hoping to breath you in. Just a small scent is all I want now. But this is a foolish dream from a foolish Heart. I don't need to hope such thoughts because I already know where my Heart is. It is home with you. It always is and it always will be. It is home remodeling Shakera's room. It is home placing dolphin wallpaper upon Devon's room walls so his love can be as free. It is assembling Channing's new bike for his birthday. And It is lying on the couch watching TV and massaging your feet after a long day. Yes my Heart is always home with you even when this body is someplace at sea in this small world.

FORGETTING WORK

Work or kissing? Hard decision. I work all day and think about work all night. What else is there to do. But just once I kissed and kissed and kissed. I closed my eyes and no longer thought of work. I thought of floating upon the clouds. I thought of traveling through tainted waves. My Heartbeat increased and my pulse slowed down. I became alive again. I became what I love. I kissed and I kissed and I kissed. Again and again. I no longer thought of work. I no longer felt stress. I became full of tears of happiness. I finally smiled the same smile that I had hidden inside from a simple long lasting kiss. I will still work all day but at night I now will think of kissing, especially that long lasting kiss from the HeartSender

THOSE WORDS

You don't know what it does to me each time I read or hear the words "I love You" from you. It makes my body tingle with the worse case of goose bumps and I float away. Even out here at sea you break me down to my knees just by a simple whisper of your love. I can see you so clear and enticing with beauty. How could I ever stop loving you. I am the one who is lucky. I have something I want to ask you but I wanted to ask in person. I have been gone for so long and I want to start over when I get back. I want so much to renew my vows with you. Yes I want to marry again. Just you, me and the kids in front of your uncle. I hope he is still preaching. Yes, I want to tell you again how much I love you in the vows. You are the only one for me and I want to make that clear again and again. It felt great saying I do the first time and I want to hear you say it again. Take this strong man into your arms again and hear him devote his life to you with all of his Heart. He is your HeartSender and your are his Sindra.

GETTING LOST WITH THE HEART

I have imagined you each night down in my arms as I held you tight. Telling you all of my childhood joys and teenage secrets. I imagine you asking me to love you forever as I gracefully accepted. I imagine you and I in a long lasting kiss. You are the one for me. I always knew that and always is like an eternity waiting to be released from a dream to reality. Systasoljah, come away with me into a world that never sleeps yet the dream never dies. A world where walking on the clouds is just as common as walking upon the pulses of a timid Heart as each beat guides you to another awaiting a soft beat. Come and love me and find what your inner self and alter ego directs you to. Come and imagine getting lost with the HeartSender.

YOUR HEARTSENDER

I am the HeartSender in true form
Taking your mind away
From the chaos of your daily norm
I will take you to places like never before
As you yearn daily
For me to give you just a little bit more
There is more to life than the physical side
I offer you a different world
Into the desire you desperately hide
So come away with me and surrender
Sit back and fall in love
With your one and only HeartSender

MIGRATING SOUTH WITH THE HEART

Your lips are cold
As I kiss you there
The Bird in me
Awakes from a nightmare
It begins to beg
And prance to no beat
Wanting you more and more
Kissing you down to your feet
Migration has finally come
And southern warmth in mind
Knowing the directions
As your body begins to unwind
I leave your lips
And fly to each breast
Chirping upon each nipple
As your treasure twitch from its deep rest
I begin to prey
Upon the soft curves
Giving you those feelings
You rightfully deserve
My hands reach
For a little bit more
As now your insides
Begins to joyfully soar
I kiss you there
And every where
Bringing emotions
Your Heart can't bare
Southern still
My goals fall into place
As the agony becomes so clear
Upon your tender flush face
Past your belly
Into a forest of tasty hairs
My tongue becomes the bird,
Lost searching without care
Oh To taste the fruit
And finding the warmth it seeks

Heartsender

As I am down on my knees
Becoming ever so weak
Deeper and Deeper
My tongue goes in
As the migrating bird
Finds its nest to win
As your hands
Forcefully grab my ears
I look up and see
Those faithful running tears
Letting me know
How this journey of the bird feels
As I always knew
That your love was real
It came to be
A southern trip to render
As you will always want and think of
Your one and only HeartSender

END OF THE ROAD

At the end of the road I see your beautiful face As the day turn into night Your smile makes my heart race Yes this truck I drive So often in a week Leads me to you and your eyes Into that glimpse of love I seek A dirty old man I don't claim to be Yet a dreamer of romance In my own little fantasy So please don't look away Or take any offense Of the smiles and eye winks From my Soul each passing instance

WANTS AND NEEDS

What you want and what you need Can be the same thing But are you prepared here and now To let The Heart make your soul sing? Come if you will my sweet pretender And feel all of the erotic passion From your one and only HeartSender

<u>WAITING</u>

Even in the dark I've seen your tears Waiting, wanting for someone like me To always be near I knew you were in pain Thinking of him and the love You offered but never gained You wanted his touch and faithful hand Yet I was there to give you the love Your body and Heart could never stand DC Live was where we met As I looked into your eyes And saw the inner woman My soul will never forget But I will never lead you astray And promise you that the love I offer will always stay All I know is what I now feel Remembering your moist lips and tender body That makes this broken Heart heal. Yolanda, It is I to you who shall surrender As I now claim to be your one and only HeartSender

DISTANT KISS

She blows me a kiss across the miles Driving my insides crazy Just to vision her tender smile Lifting me higher and higher Adding fuel to my soul And unending internal fire Just from her free willing distant kiss Gives me the support and comfort I knew that I will always miss

UNEEK BLK BU T

Pure
Untouched
Endless
You see in me
What you can't conceive
I walk in the shadows
Of your confused mind
The beauty in me
Stays upon your mind
The color so deep
Blurs the path to your soul
A strength unmatched
In any known time
Carried a race
Through a struggle
Inhuman to the Heart
I am Uneek Blk Bu T

It is not the color
That makes me unique
Nor the desire of my body
That you seek

I stand alone
Upon a Threshold forsaken
As now the knowledge of the Black Queen
Is needfully Awakened

I carry in me
A passion so tender
Encouraging the strong black man
To never ever surrender

It is I that mends
The child's silent cry
And consoles the tears
Each man tries to hide

Heartsender

I take the long nights
And ignore the need for sleep
To ensure the love of the Black family
Will in time forever keep

If the want exists
I tend to satisfy
Giving you the ecstasy
You can never deny

I am more than a woman
That will stay by your side
I am the gleam that will never disappear
In each closed eye

You will think of me
As time will stand still
And know a love
That truly feels real

I am that partner in time
That you seek
I am forever
Your Uneek BlkBu T

THE PERFECT LIFE

The perfect life is the one I live
As each day I see the many gifts
God has to graciously give
I tend to see strength in faith
Striving for my dreams
And the goals we prematurely make
I love my life from the good to the bad
Overcoming all obstacles
That leaves others helpless and sad
Yes I live the perfect life
A little different than my childhood dream
But it is the strength inside
That wipes my tears clean

STARLIT GAME

Maria,
I stand two inches taller
Looking down into your eyes
I possess 105 pounds more muscle
As It is your love taken by surprise
I live only an hour
From the touch of your hand
And I've bared only nine years more
Of life, in loves final stand
Curious you may be
Of this man's passionate Heart
And Curious you may be
Of that one unending dying art
But it is I who is weak
After traveling each desolate mile
From the grace of your vision
And forever heavenly smile
Even from a picture
You have me to claim
As I plant your love
In an eternal starlit game
To answer your questions
I have this to say
I have a dog named Bear
And a son who will always with me stay
His name is Channing
He is eleven years of age
And his mom is in Cleveland
Happy with life and engaged

<u>OF HER</u>

    I see love as being much more than words can describe. I tend to try to explain what makes me shake at the thought of holding her. I tend to try to explain what I crave day in and day out. I wake to the thought of her. I wake to the memory of her. I wake to the knowledge that my Heart nourishes from her love. The passion and ecstasy that she gives me is unexplainable. The desires that I feel for her can never be for another. Love is such a small word for such deep, deep, deep emotions that she gives me. The thought of her lips upon mine only tortures me with despair that the dream will never be reality. Over and over and over again I feel her eyes piercing through my soul even when they can't be seen. That is how I perceive this thing they call love

WHAT YOU NEED FROM ME

I can go deep into your mind as well as deep into your body. I can take you there emotionally and physically. I can have your world spinning around as you max over and over and over again. You will nourish from the thought of making love to me. You will call out my name even when I am not around. The mere thought of me would make you moist where you are. Your body will be mine to explore from top to bottom. I will taste your treasure anytime of the day. You will yearn to be with me emotionally and physically.

That is what you need from me.

I EXIST

But I do exist. I eat, drink, and think only of Love. I dream of finding her, that Angelic Queen, for me to serve each and every moment. I am merely a peasant prepared to become a Knight to protect her with this strong tender body. I cook, Clean, and consume the ways of love. But first I must find her. Could it be you?

THE RIGHT ONE?

Well to answer your question
I shall give it a good try
But the love in your own heart
Should never make you cry

The right one is always with you
Deep down inside
Caressing you and loving you
As the night goes by

But you must open your eyes
To a love that is new
And be patient and wait
For that one love that is true

You will have many lonely nights
But be strong
And never settle for anything less
Than your Heart's God given right

Free to love that one special man
Giving you all the love
His heart and soul
Can withstand

You will know when that one love has appeared
For he will hold you and caress you
With passion for all of your dying years.

PATIENT MAN

I am patient and will never settle for less than true love. I search for someone who I can truly love and never wonder in body and in mind to another. I look for that one special lady who I can cook for and serve each night with body massages and long talks of my childhood dreams. I look for that one special lady who would support me mentally in times of need and in times when I have no need for support. She must make me smile at the weirdest moments just from the thought of her. And when I reach for her she will be willing just as I will be willing anytime of the day. Each time we part she will know my feelings for her and each time we are together she will know How much she means to me. So I wait with patience because I was promised that one day I will fall in deep unforgettable Heart stopping breathtaking never-ending love.

YOU'RE HOOKED

No! You're wrong
That is not what really occurred.
I made you weak with passion
And now your senses are blurred
What really happened
Was total ecstasy
From your want
To always have me
Each time your Heart
Skipped each faithful beat
Was reminding you
Of love's deniable defeat
You want me
And the desires that I hold
As the discomfort in your life
Slowly and timely unfolds
For I bring you hope
With each fallen tear
As your soul stands up
To your Heart's only fear
So give in!
To the love I now give
And let your own passions
Faithfully and forever now live.

<u>MORE</u>

But can I be more? More of the man you need? More
of the man you seek? Can I be your every thought? Your
every whisper of love? Can I be there when your body
aches? When you reach for someone to touch each part
of you? Can I be more than just a thought or dream?
More than a vision you've never seen? Can I be your
private cook? Private dancer? Private fantasy? Can I
be more than just a one night stand? More than just
gossip with the girls? More than just your pleasure
pool of ecstasy? Can I be just a little bit more?

ONE NOTE STAND

This was more than just a one note stand
This was ME being that forever kind of man
You brought out a side of me
I yearned to always see
And if you go away
I will lose my own reality
And drift into a world of total make-believe
Constantly remembering each of your gentle words
Thinking of giving you a love you rightfully deserve
Yes this was more than just me and you
This was a revelation of love
That will forever be true.

COME

What you want and what you need Can be the same thing But are you prepared here and now To let The Heart make your soul sing? Come if you will my sweet pretender And feel all of the erotic passion From your one and only HeartSender

PRETEND FOR ME

Natalia,
I have a favor to ask
As this year
Comes to a slow end
And all of my hurt
And pain begins to set in
From the memory
Of all my loneliness
And love lost to despair
I just need a friend
To tell me that she cares
Pretend for me
That it is I that you love
And need forever more
To wipe this year's final tears
Out that lonely door
Just pretend that my touches
And gentle kisses
Will be on your mind
As those final seconds
Loses 2001 for all of time
Pretend that I am there
Making sweet love to you
Under the hidden moon's light
And that you want me again and again
To caress your body tight
Pretend that my whispers
Are bringing chills
Down your spine
And that my foreplay
Brings a passion
That is divine
So Natalia
Just this once
As this year comes to a close
Please be a pretender
For your one and only
HeartSender

<u>MY UNINHIBITED ONE</u>

I see you
Beyond your long silky hair
And knee weakening eyes
I see you
Beyond your pearly red lips
And perfectly sculptured physique
My Uninhibited One
I read your poetry
And became lost
In my own dream
In my own fantasy
Wanting to be the one
You wrote of
Wanting to be the one
Inspiring each deep word
And each Heart throbbing touch
My Uninhibited One
I see you
Beyond those words upon your page
I see you
Lying beside me
As I touch each part of you
With first my opened eyes
Remembering,
And never forgetting
Your smile,
Your curves
My Uninhibited One
If only you knew
What lies beyond these words
The power the emotions possess
The power true love shall confess
My Uninhibited One
The depth of your treasure
I shall taste

Heartsender

> The depth of pleasure
> You shall know in haste
> My Uninhibited One
> You shall know all of me
> Your one and only
> Forever HeartSender

MASSAGING THE MIND

Let me give you a quick mind massage from the Heart.
As tender as you make me feel
Is as tender as my love is real
Come and see
What true love can really be
Just close your eyes
And prepare for a Heart stopping surprise
As you enter a world
That will make your soul twirl
And prepare to surrender
To your one and only HeartSender

A NATURAL POET

A Natural Poet has that internal gift
Bringing words to life
That the dying Heart does truly miss
Into the scattering stars your mind will soon be
As they bring your dreams to reality
So come away with me and forever surrender
Into the tender exotic words of your one and only
HeartSender

LISALOVELY

Holy Sh**! I opened your page
And took a deep breath.
You had the body of a goddess
And the face I will never forget
Forgive me LisaLovely
But I now to you surrender
And swear to always be
Your one and only HeartSender

TRUSTING THE HEART

For you, Each promise I now make
Will be Stolen words
From my Hearts Eternal Case
I am not just a man
With words of silver and gold
Yet a man who will be by your side
As each night grows old
Trust me and know that I am no pretender
When I say that I will always be
Your one and only HeartSender

<u>ANATH'S HEART</u>

Anath's inner Heart
Is what I seek
Caressing and kissing
As her knees become weak
Into her mind I shall remain
As this goddess of love and sex
Bares the soul I shall tame
Anath It is with you I now plead
Come into the Lair of Hearts
And gather all you will ever need

HAITAN QUEEN

I am doing great Sweetteaspoon,
My Haitian Forever Queen
Just standing by in despair
Ready to show you what true love really means
For all the world is a playground of despair
For lovers who chose no longer to ever again care
But it will be this queen from far away
To show me that love will forever stay

THE FINER THINGS IN LIFE

You want to be held when times are tough
You want that special someone to always trust
You want to dine in happy tears
You want that special friendship to last through the years
You want that quiet intimate evening conversation
You want that deep spiritual religious revelation
You want that occasional morning breakfast in bed
You want that laughter from the silly things that he said
You want all these finer things in life
That money and gold can never offer to Heart's eternal light

<u>RELEASE</u>

The Heart is simple yet so complex
He has so many dreams and deep goals that he has set
He is more than a Marine (:))
As you may now know
His Heart is with the Navy
Which he joined so long ago.
He will be releasing a book
From his deep ongoing mind
That will stay in most Hearts
For all of time
With him the poetry flows at will
From simple thoughts of love
Through this abandoned dark hill
I love the fact the you have high goals to reach
Leaving lost dreams for others to teach
But the Heart wants to further Feast
So tell me much more
Of what your Heart has to release.

IN SERENITY

The day has come
I have found my forever one
February 9th two zero zero zero
So much pain yet many happy tears
As I birth a love to last through the years
In Serenity I found what I live for
In Serenity I thank God for upping his score
In Serenity I live each day out right
In Serenity I dine in her Eternal light
My Sweet daughter I give you my love and life
To always know that your mom will never give up the fight
To protect you and shelter you
From harms way
It will be my protecting Heart
That you shall know
Will forever and always stay.

<u>ADMIRING THE HEARTSENDER</u>

The Heart is the person I keep down inside
Who comes alive bringing out the emotions and feelings
I desperately hide
It is he I look upon and truly admire
As he graces those thoughts that can lite any Heart on
fire
But he is still a major part of me
Bringing to life my every fantasy
And it is the Heart that will make you surrender
And never deny that he will be
Your one and only HeartSender.

LONGING

I've seen the ocean
Endless without a beginning
I've danced to its melody
So soft and compelling
I've felt each water drop
Full of happy longing tears
I've seen the Ocean
I've felt all of it's beauty
But I long to feel you.

UNSEEN SMILE

Unseen smile
I give into you
Your quiet plead
And unjust temper
You take me
All of me
Far, far away
Off into a whole new world
Where you and I
Are all that sing
This life's quiet melody
Unseen smile
Come and claim
What is rightfully yours
Come and mold a masterpiece
Of Love, Of pleasure,
Of Everlasting Ecstasy
Unseen smile
You have all that I truly need
You have what makes me, me
You have the curious Heart
Of the one and only HeartSender

IMMORTALITY

Immortality
That is what I give
For all the Hearts
I shall outlive
Come and forever see
That my love
Is of Immortality
Kissing you slow
And never letting go
Taking you there
Showing that I care
Deep inside
In one slow stride
Up and down
Spinning your world around
As you shall smile
In each love mile
I shall retain
The love we shall gain
Immortality

<u>ALMOST 4 AM</u>

I couldn't sleep
I tried so hard
It's late
It's early
You're not here
The evening rain
Has turned into
Morning rain
But I am tired
From a midnight run
Just a touch
No!
Just a kiss
Of your tender lips
To hold you
To caress you
To be all that you want
Me to always be
Your hands searching
Your mind speaking
Your love living
Only visions
I have of you
Only memory
Only lost touches
Only missed wishes
Come and take me
Into your loving arms
And know why I
Will always be
Your one
And only
HeartSender
Loving you still
At almost 4am
Come and believe
In true love
True ecstasy

NETTING A FRIEND

I hear what you say
But my friend's list does not reflect
Where in my Heart you stay
I travel the net with an open eye
Only pursuing a Heart
I can never deny
It is true I wrote that poem for a stranger
Who's eyes and lips
Places my soul in danger
It could have been only for you
But that would be a lie
You knew was not true
Instead I wrote for the woman in my dream
A woman I never held
Nor have ever seen
So for her I just reach for each night
Hoping Her touch will end this fight
And so I awake in an empty bed
As my reality has been misled
But I would love to have you as a friend
And promise It would last until time will dreadfully
end

<u>ALL HANDS ON ME</u>

All hands on me
If that is the kind of woman you are
But I must warn you
I can take my love ever so far
I can come correct in your every fantasy
As you will always yearn for the mere touch of me
So bring your hands and every desire
And let the HeartSender
Lite your erotic world on fire

PRETENDER

Well you talk a good game
But talking and making love
Is and never will be the same
For once I am inside
And you begin to ride
You will finally truly feel
My erotic sex appeal
I will cover you with pleasure
As I taste your fruitful treasure
And then you shall beg
As I spread apart each leg
Waiting to hear your moans
The way I've always known
So keep talking as a pretender
As you dream of your one and only
HeartSender

<u>MORNING REACH</u>

I woke up this morning and reached for you but all I touched was the memory of your gentle skin. I lost my breath and sanity with the dying assurance of a false reality. Why weren't you here to hold and kiss. Instead I awoke to emptiness. I would have made you breakfast in bed. I would have showered you with all of my love. I would have given the morning love you need, giving you all of me. But an empty bed is all I have with all the love and desire for you branded in my head.

Your one and only HeartSender

MY EROTIC QUEEN

Now look here My Erotic Queen
Do you really know what Pleasure truly means
I will taste you ever so slow
Grabbing those hips
And never letting go
As my tongue goes deep inside
Taking your body on one hell of a ride
And just when you couldn't take any more
I am still between lose legs
More than doubling your score
As you may know this Heart doesn't play
As I give you pure satisfaction All through the day
Deep into your sweet ginger
It will be I tasting you deeply
As Your one and Only HeartSender

YOUR PROMISE!

    See, that is your problem! You promise me a feeling that will last for days. I need a feeling that will last me a lifetime. I want to look back on the First time we make love and say to myself "Damn what a night". I want to dream of that night before and after it happens. And It will Happen!!! I want to be nervous before and nervous afterward from the thought of will it ever happen again. I want to shake in my shoes as you slowly remove your shirt. I want to become weak in the knees from the first time I see your bare breast. I want to scream from deep down in my Soul from the first time I am deep in your treasure going in and out then in and out then in and out over and over and over again. I want to become lost in that dream before we make love and want to never ever find myself after we make love. Any one will see how lost I am just walking in my own dream each day thinking of making love to you. The depth of your sweet tasty womanhood is all I could ever dream of and yet YOU Only want this feeling to last for a couple of Days!!! While I want it to Last and always last for a Lifetime!!!!

MATCHED

We were matched together
From those at BP
So I guess I will tell you
Just a little bit about me
I live in Dahlgren, VA
Alone with my Son
And am in search of you
So our Hearts can become one
I will give you my picture
If it is what you ask
And to mold your smile
Will be my primary task
So kick back a note
And tell me what's on your mind
And jump start a friendship
That will last for all of time.

ABOUT ME

About Me?
I am different
Kind
Sensual
I feel deep
I can be erotic
I can be sensitive
I can be strong
I sometimes drift away
Off into another world
I have been all over the world
I have been to Japan
Singapore, Thailand,
Hong Kong, Australia,
Europe
And many more
I am Navy
But to really know me
You must open your eyes
To something new
Something addictive
Something you never thought
That you would ever find
So about Me
You shall know
You shall feel
You shall never forget.

THE EMOTIONS INSIDE

I am not a Poet, even though I may rhyme
For the words I utter, shall now pause time
Open up your Heart and see what is inside
And release that true person you desperately hide
And come away with me, to a land you once knew
And find that one special love that is true
An Emotionalist is what I now claim
With passion others wish to somehow tame
It is the true me you cannot bare
For I know how to show I truly care
Love, No! That is not what you desire
You want ecstasy setting your soul on fire
You want what my words now give
You want my emotions to forever in you live
So I now tell you to close each blinking eye
And see the beauty in your own Emotions inside

WHAT I SEE

I walk out and look up to the graying sky
I see the stars, not yet formed
I see her face, that I have never seen
I see life, but I have never lived
I see the waves, yet never swam
I see my tears, yet I have never cried
I see pain, yet I can never bleed
I see the falling angels, yet am without faith
I see the rain, but no clouds
I see the floating feather, yet no wind
I see drifting melody, yet no song plays
I see her smile, yet It was I who took that smile away
For what I see is a man not yet a man
Until he has claimed true love
I see a passionate soul, yet no love to claim

THE SINGLE LIFE'S TRUTH

Ok this is the truth
I shall tell
The reason
Behind my loneliness
Not letting anyone in
Not allowing to be loved
Yes I am full of love
Full of most women's dreams
I seem to be that perfect man
Faithful and loving
That is what I am
But love again I cannot
I am trapped
In chambers
That has no escape
Eleven Damn years
Since last we kissed
Eleven years of nightmares
Waking to a lost touch
To this day
It is so clear
How I held her
A fool!!! Am I
To let her go
As this tear falls
I must admit
Defeat
Of this Heart
I reach for her
But no hand to kiss
Others tried
But no success
I shielded my Heart
With hopes of anew
Moments ago she called
The same sweet voice
But not asking for me
Yet for her son

Heartsender

I froze like always
I stuttered like before
My mind went blank
I rehearsed what to say
A thousand times
"Forgive me woman,
You are the one I love!"
But all that came out
Was simply
"He is not here"
As the phone hung up
I cursed out loud
Why!! Damn it!!!
Why!!!
Ok, I am better
The emotions have left my mind
And I shall try again
Another hopeful time
Yes I shall find
A love that is true
And live my life
Happily all the way through
That teenage love
That turned into Heartbreak
Shall not instill in my life
An eternal Heartache
Like time has promised
It shall happen soon
When the pain will disappear
From the next full moon
So that is my story
The reason that I claim
A single bachelor's life
With a Heart that cannot be tamed.

WHY CAN'T IT BE

And why can't it be that way
Aren't we mortal
Of flesh and bones
So love should come some day

We should have happiness too
Live, laugh, dream
And see the hard times through

So why can't we make it be
That every dream
Can be our on little reality

UPON FIRST SIGHT

Upon First Sight,
I ponder on what to do
Scared
Nervous
My Heart races
CreoleRed will soon come
Moments
Upon endless moments
My Heart races to beyond
My mind breathes only chaos
What do I do?
Do I grab her into my arms
And kiss eternity into her soul
Do I drop to my knees
Begging her to forever stay?
Do I just let it flow
Let the words we shared
Turn into reality
No more fantasy
No more walking dreams
CreoleRed shall come to me
With a kiss
With a tear
With all I can ever be

BUT THERE IS MORE

But there is more CreoleRed
So much more
Of tender words
You never heard before
I can tell you
All of my dreams
And have your insides
Turning into sweet cream
But with you
I am a different man
Releasing emotions
The best way I can
I come to you
With open arms
Letting you know
That I will bring you no harm
You see what you did?
To this big strong guy
You gave him new life and love
His Heart can never deny

AN EROTIC ART

I am with you staring you down
Plotting on ways to love you
With this new passion that I have found
Come to me and reveal what you seek
And know Why I make your Heart
Ever so weak
You will be mine
Until love do us part
And I shall be yours
Fulfilling this eternal erotic art.

WAKING TO YOU

Well I woke up and I guess I was still dreaming because you were lying next to me wearing nothing but a sleeping smile. I just stared at your dark eyebrows and slowly moving eyes under your eyelids. I wondered what where you dreaming of. I ran my fingers through your hair and kissed your forehead as your arms came around me. I knew you were still sleep. So I drew you near me flesh to flesh and caressed your body with my body. I could feel your hips moving even as you slept wanting me. I ran my hands slowly down your back as your legs began to wrap around me. But I wasn't about to make love. No not when you were sleep. I could feel your moisture upon my manhood as it rose to the occasion taunting me, begging me to enter it's new found home. So I kissed your neck as your hands ran down my back yet you were still sleep dreaming of what I wanted to do. I gently and firmly squeezed your butt forcing your hips to roll more yet you still slept. It was self torture for me. I dared not wake you like this. My lips somehow found your breast and I can hear your breathing stop then speed up as the nipples hardened So I…

COME FORTH

Well if you once wrote poetry
It never left your side
Just let go of the pain
You desperately often hide
Reach down inside
As you have done before
To find that passion
You will once again adore
Let me bring it forth
That beauty in you I seek
Just let the words flow
And make this strong man weak
Think of me and love
It will give you that helping hand
And know that ecstasy
Will make its final stand

ONE DANCE

I am sorry for not completing
The bedtime story from before
But we shall make our own
To last forever more
CreoleRed
You lit a dangerous fire
And inspired a beast
Among my lost desire
What should I do
Run and hide?
To escape the passion
I keep down inside
Florida is not
So far away
Because in your arms
I want to forever stay
What am I thinking
I must be a fool
To think someone like you
Would make me their love tool
You are a princess
Heir to an erotic throne
And I am a mere peasant
Cursed to live my life alone
But if you feel
I have a slight chance
Then take my hand
And make your love forever dance

VISUALIZE ME

Visualize me as you close each eye
And see a man who will always stand by
Loving you and touching you in so many ways
As he drops to his knees begging you to forever stay
If not for a minute then for a lifetime
As the passions in his soul you shall forever find

Visualize me and know how each muscle feels
Giving you the ecstasy your body yearns to feel
But before you feel my physical side
Open your Heart and release the emotions you hide

Visualize me and forever surrender
To the form of this man that your love shall render.

FAVORITE GYRL

Now I am at a lost for words
A mistake was made
Forgive me
And know how I plead
As I drop down
To one faithful knee
A fool I have been
To spread the love too thin
And failed to claim
Your trust to win
Favorite Gyrl
You shall always be
As I strive to find
My eternal destiny
For now a friend
I now crave
And hopefully never again
To misbehave
I have been to Hawaii
As you now travel
As the worldly beauty
Begins to unravel
This sailor man
Needs your forgiving hand
As his Favorite Gyrl
Makes him a forever kind of man

MY POETIC SOUL

A glimpse of beauty I see
Uplifting
Carrying me further away
From all I know as reality
Your passion
Your glow
I can't deny
In your eyes
The windows
The gateway
Of your Poetic Soul

MEMORIAL DAY EVE

The day comes to an end
I'm tired, confused
I look over to an empty couch
By a wall that shields
An empty bed
But when the sun rises
I shall celebrate
Being a Navy man
I shall remember
All of those before me
Who sailed the endless seas
Giving up their own freedom
I shall remember
Their lonely nights
Standing the watch
I now stand
Missing the kisses
I now miss
I shall cherish
Their courage
To leave behind
Their lover's touch
To trust their Heart
Will remain true
Yes this Memorial Day
I shall remember
The sailors I follow
Through the Arabian Gulf
I sailed as well
Through the Philippine Sea
I also conquered
Through the Sea of Japan
I fought the endless typhoons
I shall remember
I shall cherish
For I am a sailor
Who sailed the seven Seas
Around this world

Heartsender

Leaving behind
The touch of someone beautiful
Dreaming of you
Wanting you
Fighting for you
Upon this Memorial Day Eve

<u>LUCKY</u>

You have one lucky husband I must say again and again
He has the chance to touch you tenderly
And has your Heart to win
I wish I was that lucky of a guy
To have someone like you to make love to as the nights
go by

<u>WANT ME TO BE?</u>

Well who do you want me to be?
I can be that friend
You reach for in times of stress
I can be that special guy
With eyes you tend to undress
I can be that lover
You desire time and time again
I can be that soulmate
Who will be with you always
Until the end
So who do you Ms. Thang
Want me to be?

OLDEST ART

I dance upon the tear
Your words made me shed
And here upon this night
Your love I faithfully wed
It is true a rhyme
Can't reflect upon the Heart
Yet it nourishes
From the worlds oldest art:
Love, with all of it's fallacies
We caress and embrace
Escaping the soul's jealousy
So come away with me
Into a world you shall always reign
And lose all control
From what your Heart shall gain

MIDNIGHT YEARNING

It is Midnight
And I am in that mood
You know the one
As our bodies begin to move
But you're not here
You are oh so far away
As all of my desires
Awakes and begins to play
I vision you in nothing but a smile
Calling for me
Across that never ending mile
"Take me Now! If you dare"
Such soft demands
Ones that my passion can't bare
I become insane or half crazy
Reaching for you, calling for you
As reality becomes a little hazy
As the clock strikes twelve upon this night
It is I who has failed again
This longing for you I now fight

WHAT YOU DON'T WANT

You don't want to know me. Not the true me. Because you will get lost in a world you can't escape. Your dreams would consume me. Your desires will always yearn for me. Everywhere you go you will think of me. I am not one that you want to know because your mind will turn in circles losing all sense of direction not knowing which way to turn. For I love deep but I fail to love now. I fail to find a Heart as pure as mine willing to go that extra distance into a happy place where we depend on nothing but love. My every word would be her gospel just as her every wish will be what I live for. You don't want to know me because I am one who is never forgotten.

IMMORTAL LOVE

Our Next Life. We are already immortal. I see us loving each other in the afterlife. As we long for immortality. We kiss when the feelings are right. We make love when the feeling is needed. We give each other pleasures that words can't describe. I tend to your needs as if It was all that mattered to me. I kiss you there over and over and over again. As you beg for this immortal touch. I send a feeling that your spine gives to your hips as you roll with my southern kisses giving me more of your tender treasure. I taste the fruits for which you bare to the last drop. Your immortal passions take control as you beg for more. I taste, I tease, I please. My immortal love is all that you will ever need.

<u>DESPERATE LOVE</u>

I am desperate to love someone from deep down inside
And show them all the beauty I desperately hide
Because there is so much beauty I keep within
Searching for that one who has my eternal love to win
I will love her right with all the passion I hold
As in her trusting arms the world will see true love
unfold
So I guess you can say that I am a desperate man
Who will love some lucky woman more than her Heart can
ever stand

THE ECSTASY IN YOU

You want a man to hold too
But have you looked inside
At the ecstasy in you?
Can you come to me
And answer my cry
As I yearn for your loving
As the night goes slowly by
I want a woman just the same
Kissing her, touching her
As she calls out my name
Yes, I know the desires you hold
As you wake alone
From dreams that leave you cold
You want this man and all of his pleasures
As he kisses you down
Teasing your secret treasure
But tell me sweet lady
Here and now
In your own true Heart
Does love endow?
Will you take me to that unknown land
And give me what I want
From the mere touch of your hand
You want a man to hold too
But you also want a man
Who's heart is true.

LITTLE ONE

Little One
Look for me
Smiling up to you
Pushing you
Driving you
To that place
You ought to be
That one dream
That is your reality
Against all odds
Against the drowning tears
We travel as one
My lips upon yours
My hand in your hand
Each step you make
I follow
I cherish
I am your shoulder standing by
I am your handkerchief
When you cry
A lawyer, a dream
We shall achieve
A lover, a friend
You shall receive
Little one
Fly with me
As you soar
To your destiny.

<u>YOUR STYLE</u>

I love your poem and I can relate,
But it will be I who you shall choose
As your eternal mate.
You see I can get into your mind,
And let your emotions run free
As I mold your Dreams
Into a longing reality
I can see the beauty
You have within
So I am here to inform you
That true love shall now begin
Test your skills
And creative style
Let the words run free
As your desires run wild
I can bring it out-
That passion you desperately hide
And take you to that place
Your soul can't deny
Your daughter has your beauty
And golden smile
You should be proud
Of your God given child
So hang if you can
With the words I render
As the ecstasy you harvest
To me shall forever surrender

<u>YOUR GOLDEN SMILE</u>

And I searched for you.
At just a whisper of your voice
I knew
My wait was over
I shall not snooze
I shall not hold back
I will give my all
I will make you love me
Just as I know that I will love you
Your words forms my inner Heart
That nourishes from the thought of you
No man will take away the thought
No man will even conceive trespassing
They will see the power in our love
They will see how much I need you
They will envy each kiss
I vision your love
I vision your golden smile
I vision you walking upon a cloud
Drifting
Searching
Reaching only for me
I try to imagine not meeting you
And I broke down to my knees
And prayed how could life be so cruel
But now I have found you
Life is not cruel
Yet uplifting
As my love unfurls
Into your Golden smile

SECOND INTERVIEW

The second interview is a little more difficult. It judges your self control combined with a taste test. Well It starts off as I Remove your shirt as you keep your hands to yourself. I slowly kiss your neck then down to each covered breast. I slowly remove your bra then taste what is now uncovered. Remind you it is a self-control test. I dance for a moment with my tongue upon the right then I waltz over to the left still massaging the right. I then lay you down and slowly remove your bottoms. My tongue then goes traveling to your belly button as it finds a temporary home. I then remove your panties then my tongue ventures southward once more. It swarms down to your right thigh then travels inward yet still upon the thy. As my hands begin to caress your left thigh. You spread your legs further yet keeping your hands to yourself. I then go on to the second part of the interview for the taste test. My tongue finds your secret treasure and tastes the depth of its juices taking in all of the fruits you have to offer. Over and over and over again your hips begin to roll yet you must show some type of control. You must not max you must not think about the pleasures you are receiving as I go deeper searching for the one spot testing your self control. Again you shiver. Again you call out my name. But I must warn you, You must not max. You must show some type of self-control. After a while of tasting and admiring your self-control. The interview has concluded. Would you pass the interview?

MY ANGEL

My Angel. Has left me astray
So I will go down on one knee to pray
That She will come back to me
And turn my dreams into reality
It is not fare to give up all
Just from a missed phone call
So I ask you Mighty from above
To bring back my one true love
And to make this Angel realize
That she took my soul by surprise
So please Angel, come back to me
And behold that I am your Heart's destiny

YOUR DREAM COME TRUE

I picture it just a little bit different but I do like your style. You see I am an impatient man with a patient desire. I visit you a few times wanting but withholding the urge I have for you. And each time I can see what you want and what you need. I kiss you softly with eyes closed upon the first visit. The second visit my hands begin to wonder just a little. The third visit I taste your bare breast. The fourth visit is just a little bit different. You see I already how to take you there and I do plan on taking you there slowly and keeping you there all night. I enter the room and I slowly undress you. My clothes are still on. I bathe you. Touching each part of you. I then remove my shirt. Yet you are still in the tub. I wash your breast and inner thighs and feel the heat coming from your body. I dry you off and carry you into the bedroom and lay you upon the bed. I kiss you ever so deeply and then begin to kiss your neck. I work my way down to each breast claiming what is rightfully mine. I go down further leaving a path of soft kisses upon your soft skin. I reach your belly button as my hands still caresses your breast. My tongue goes further south into your forest of hairs searching eagerly for its lost treasure. Your hips begin to roll as if it was guiding me to the unseen light. You spread your legs inviting me to the door of your eternal gift. My tongue finds your forbidden treasure and your moans escalate. Your hips begin to roll more and more. Your hands grab my head pushing me deeper and deeper into your house of pleasure. I can taste the juices coming at no end. You whisper my name and I whisper my feelings into you. Your body tightens then shakes. Your thighs clash and squeeze my head. Then you relax and I kiss my way back up. and towering over you. You reach for my pants and unbutton them then...

FIRST INTERVIEW

Yes I am still taking applications but you must answer a few questions for me. Are you willing to fall deep in love? Are you willing to make love whenever I reach for you? Are you willing to be served and treated like a queen. Are you willing to have me cook and clean for you then give you a total body massage. Are you willing to come home and have your feet rubbed as I tell you how my day at work was? Are you willing to go on shopping sprees buying the sexiest dresses? Are you willing to show the world that true love does exist? If the answer to all of these questions is yes then you have passed the first interview. If not maybe we can still chat and work out any differences.

<u>BLIND MAN</u>

He must be a fool or blind to even see
Just how many men has you as there fantasy
If you were mine I will always be by your side
Loving you and kissing you as the night goes slowly by
Keep your head up and look towards the stars
And just remember how very special and beautiful you
truly are.

YOU ARE MINE

Wait a minute!! To you I shall now explain
Your status in this life's eternal game
You see, You will forever be mine
Because it was your love I waited patiently to find
Those other guys can only envy
The emotions and desire you now have for me
It is your Heart I now claim
And it shall be your ecstasy I shall now tame
At the store or wherever you may go
The feelings for me will always show
I hope I made myself perfectly clear
That losing your love is my greatest and unwanted
fear.

YOU LOVED ME BEFORE

Yes I have had your Heart before Over and over in my dreams. You see I dreamed that you loved me but it was more than love. You nourished from my love for you just as I nourished from your love for me. In my dreams we made love like never before. I cooked for you. I cleaned for you. I massaged your body each night from head to toe. And each night I listened to your childhood dreams just as I told you mine. So in My dreams I had your love before just like tonight I will dream that dream again faithfully.

YOU WANT ME

No! You're wrong
That is not what really occurred.
I made you weak with passion
And now your senses are now blurred
What really happened
Was total ecstasy
From your want
To always have me
Each time your Heart
Skipped each faithful beat
Was reminding you
Of love's deniable defeat
You want me
And the desires that I hold
As the discomfort in your life
Slowly and timely unfolds
For I bring you hope
With each fallen tear
As your soul stands up
To your Heart's only fear
So give in!
To the love I now give
And let your own passions
Faithfully forever now live.

I WANT A WIFE

I want a wife who will always stay
And love me truly
Until her last dying day

I want a wife who will last through the night
As I will make endless love to her
Holding her body ever so tight

I want a wife, slim and in shape
So she can keep me home
Coming back to the loving we will make

I want a wife who knows how to care
And mold the ecstasy
That we both shall always share

I want a wife to make me smile
From the sweet humorous things
She learns after a great while

I want a wife, even though I shall cook and clean
And show what a strong black love
Will forever truly mean

I want a wife, could it be you
Who will find that one soul
With all the love that is true

THE WANT OF WANTING

To want is what I want
As the night turns into night again
I see only the timber falling
I see the full moon wanting to set
Shall I want even more
Shall I want what every one else wants
But I know now
No! I always knew
That what I want is just a want
Everyone wants
Even the unreachable things
I strive for what I want
The sadness sets in form of reality
As what I want becomes distant
As what I want becomes fantasy
Shall I want more
Shall I stop wanting
But I want to want
As the art of wanting to want
Becomes the only art I wake to
The art of wanting to want
Nourishes my Heart and stolen dreams
And I shall always live and reach
For my every want.

A RIGHT TO LOVE

And they said love is only for the lucky ones
I think not
For the feeling of love and all of its beauty
Has blessed not only me
But everyone
The love every Heart has yearned to feel
A father to his son
A mother to her daughter
A boy to his dog
A girl to her doll
A husband to wife
The feeling of love
The desire to be loved
The many gifts it promises
Is everyone's right
No! love is not just for the lucky ones
It is for all
And to all I give my love

BRONXBRED

Well tell me BronxBred
What emotions stir your mind
And how can the HeartSender
Help your deepest passions unwind
For what I possess
No other man can claim
The depth of each word
Driving your reality insane
So just sit back and relax
And let your body surrender
To the ecstasy
Of your one and only HeartSender

COME AND PLAY

You damn right you're in trouble
As of now it is time to begin
And play this erotic game
You know you can't ever win
Because now I am in control
As I remove the fears you wear
And touch you in places
No other man will ever dare
As my tongue tastes
Your forbidden treasure
And you scream to the pleading
Of your bodies pleasure
Then deeper and deeper
You feel all of me
As you say a mere saddle
Is my fantasy
Come Bronx, Come and play
As I make your passions
Forever stay

LOVE THEE NOT

Love thee not
This you do know
But my body
Craves you so
For your touch
I know so well
From all the times
I was under your spell
My gentle kiss
To you I shall deny
But the feel of my skin
You've earned by and by
There is no love
That claims my Heart
So I shall use yours
Then quickly part
Hurry!
Before I change my mind
And search elsewhere
For a quick hit to find
And don't think
We are together again
And that my love
Is yours to win
This is just
A temporary fix
And don't you dare
Make it go quick
Make it last
Until I am pleased
As my passions
Are in dire need
Just remember
Of this chance you got
And never forget
I Love Thee Not

TAKING CONTROL

No! I can't lay back...and let you take control
This is my stage...and I run the show
As I lift you upon my shoulders
And spread apart your thighs
With you in midair.
Bringing tears to your eyes
As I stand erect tasting your treasure
Sending chills down your spine
No other feeling can measure
The more and more I begin to taste
I feel your legs around my head
Screeze with little haste
Relax!!! And don't you dare hold back
Because your body is now under my attack
I now claim your pearly part
With my tongue's forceful licks
And dare another woman
Even try to get into my Heart.

REMEMBER ME

Sit across from me
And see
Not only the smile on my face
Yet pure ecstasy
I am more
Than you can perceive
I am pleasure, pain,
And what your Heart shall envy
Each curve of my body
Each muscle that I bare
Shall be yours one day
If you can prove to me
That you will always care
Not only for what you see
But even the things that I hide
For one day I will need you
And In your arms I may cry
But being a man
Who should show no fear
But only in his woman's arms
Does that rule disappear
So take a mental image
And bring my body to art
In just a few moments
We shall temporarily part
But remember that image
For I may not ever return
Because life has its strange games
Even with the love that we yearn

KARAMEL KISS

Breathe away
I say to myself
As I yearn
Need
Desire your kiss
But not just the feel
Not just the taste
Not just the passion
Yet the promise
The promise of another
Even after the first
For the sweetness of Karamel
The luring of satisfaction
The depth behind the feeling
I crave so deeply
I could feel your lips
Upon my soul
Driving my sanity away
As I become nomadic
As I become what I fear
As I become Addicted
To your Karamel Kiss

OF THE POET

But I am now hiding, or so it seems, The simple words I give to you is far from the extreme. I dance upon the thought, of how it should be, and caress the wonders of my own fantasy. For others this seems like such a hopeless task, yet for me it is all of reality I shall ever ask. So about the man you wonder of now and then, and about the dreams of from whence his world now spins, There lies a place where everyone shall be the guest, and happiness in their Hearts shall be his life's quest.

<u>DYING BREED</u>

I search endlessly
But they are nowhere to be found
As my Heart approaches
That deadly ground
Where could they be,
The single true African Queens
To light up my desires
My passions never seen
I searched this world
With hopes to one day find
Just one
To ease my restless mind
To let her know
That it is her that I need
And to revamp the myth
Of a dying breed
With these strong arms
I will tightly grasp
What most men fail
To make their primary task
I will shelter her and protect her
From the hunter's prowl
And make her ecstasy
Faithfully forever howl
We shall harvest
An eternal love nest
Where others search
To bring their fears to rest
I feel my mind
Drawing you near
As I caress you gently
Wiping each unwanted tear
So where are they
To fulfill my every need
As my Heart yearns
For that Dying Breed

TALENTED ONE

No! You are the talented one
Graceful
Alluring and full of wonders
With thieving eyes
And a tempting smile
A talent that can't be matched
You play upon the emptiness
You dance upon the hopelessness
You sing upon the relentless
Upon your stage
You capture
An audience of souls
As we watch, listen
And dream
Of the passion
You have to give
I applaud your style
Your own vision of love
An agent of laughter
An agent of ecstasy
I long to one day be
For in your arms
You entertain my fears
Of how a love should be
Talented one
I have, I will always
I can never deny
That I am yours.

<u>SWEET SENSATION</u>

Ahhh but you say your Heart
Can never hold
A love for me
To faithful mold
But In the depth
Of your yearning soul
Is the existence of desire
I shall forever control
True, a poet
You now boldly claim
But the words from your Heart
I shall now tame
Look beyond the boundaries
Of your own imagination
And let your passion play
In my sweet sensation

<u>RIGHTEOUS QUEST</u>

A Quest?
A thought?
A feeling?
Should I dwell upon your tears
Wanting
Needing
Reaching for only me
Blurred vision
Dances with your mind
There is no other
There is no other man
It is only I
Strong
Willing
Possessive
Controlling
I dare not venture away from love
I see in you my need
My wants
My destiny
My sweet Poet
Compose your masterpiece
As my nomadic Heart
Begins its Righteous Quest

RETURNING

I shall come back
But only in your Heart to stay
For there is no other place
My love would ever want to lay
In you is where
My passion's love shall remain
Loving you in ways
That drives your ecstasy insane
Each gentle kiss I give to you
Shall mend each broken promise
Your Heart subdued
Yes I shall come back
To you and only you
As the sun shall rise
Shining my love through

A DANCE CALLED LOVE

Shall we dance
To our own melody
Shall we step
Into our own little fantasy
Holding each other
As the music plays
Into each other's eyes
'Til our dying days
Shall we dance
In each other's caress
And know that the desire
Is only ours to possess
As our song plays
To no nearing end
It is the movement of our passion
Where eternity shall begin
Dance away,
For I am all feet
As I stumble into your arms
As the music is silenced from my Heartbeat
But we still dance
And Hold each other tight
For this Dance called love
Is our soul's given right

KNOWING

But we do know each other
If not in flesh
Then from a dream
If not from a kiss
Then from a fantasy
Our Hearts Seen
To know someone
And to call them a friend
Is the same introduction
From a stranger
Who will be there for you
'Til the end.
We know each other

WHAT MAKES A WOMAN

It is not the age that makes the man
It is not the beauty
That turned you into a woman
It is the grace of his moves
And the tenderness you seek
It is the smile on her face
And the words that make you weak

THE LION'S DEN

In the heat of passion
I failed to introduce
The essence of my being
That your eyes seduced
I am the One
The immortal Lion King
And you are the savior
The precious Lioness Queen
But in this place
That we dwell
Lies a love story
That only time can tell
For the animalistic ecstasy
That we make
Causes loves deepest fears
To finally wake
Fear of true love
Truly being made
As the loneliness and pain
Slowly dyingly fades
This jungle of dreams
Of our reality
Is what mortals
Would call a simple fantasy
For in the Lion's Den
There is you by my side
As I get lost in the depth
Of the tenderness in your eyes
Filling that void
You once claimed
As you growl out to the world
The flavor of my name
My Lioness Queen
Come to me
And show no fear within
As we shall escape from chaos
In the Lion's Den

A SWEET MOTHER'S DAY

You bore my child
And I will never forget
The good times and bad times
Our Hearts did submit
For all in a lifetime
You stayed by my side
Taking care of my child
Even in times I made you cry
Your strength and unselfishness
I shall always admire
For you bonded this family
Even in times our Hearts tire
Though I never upon your finger
Placed that eternal ring
You still gave me the melody
My soul shall forever sing
So here I am
Down on one knee
Asking you, begging you
To give me eternity

HAPPY MOTHER'S DAY

INTO SPRING COMES LOVE

As the winter nights have come to an end
It is love from the Heart
That has come to move in
He waited so long for the snow to melt
To give you those emotions
That will be deeply felt
Though he can please you physically
He wants you to know
That spring love will control you mentally.
He will remind you each and every day
That his love will be in your Heart
To forever and ever stay
Kissing you is what he had craved
But his Heart this spring
Will be yours to enslave
Whispers of love will pour down
As the flowers bloom all around
Come and feel the wrath he renders
And know deep down why he is your
One and only HeartSender

AFTER THE VALENTINE LOVE MAKING

Staring down
Into the windows of your soul
As my sweat danced upon yours
There upon this special night
We embraced love
We embraced eternity
No words were needed
No smiles forced
No emotions explained
We both were lost into each other
No clock to give away
The passing time
Or the lost loneliness
We held each other
In a dream come true
Just staring into each others Heart
Searching for a home
Searching for a bed without tears
The silence sung our new favorite song
As our bodies remained as one
No movement
No intentions to be moved
We were the night
We were the love to be envied
We were Valentines
And after the love making
We wore happy tears from eternity

WHY YOU?

Because you have beauty that captures the eye. A beauty that any man can see that begins from inside. You tend to dream yet to most you are their angel they seek, You tend to imagine a true love your Heart can keep. A trendsetter you claim as others follow your lead, yet you answer to only a higher need. So you deserve this poem and many more to come, As I shall make your reality and dreams join as one

BASTARD CHILD

Life is not always a fairytale
And never written
Where love will always prevail
Even in the darkest hour
When two truly doubt
Love's God given power
Sometimes Hearts go astray
And two may wonder
Even as they lay
A child comes and the man runs scared
Neglecting his honor
For the child he bares
But later in life he finally realizes
His responsibilities
When the true need arises
And becomes a man strong and bold
Taking his woman
Nourishing the love she holds
Begging forgiveness to never leave
And raise the child they both conceived
Though a bastard at birth
The child now has a father
Upon this earth

<u>MAKING ME</u>

Who I am?
Is of little concern
But who you want me to be
Is what I truly yearn
For I am your desire
A simple erotic flare
Offering you pleasure
Your soul can't bare
I tend to want
Even the things unseen
I tend to nourish
From your love machine
So tell me tender lady
Of eyes from a fantasy
Tell me who do you
Want me to be?

TRUE LIFE

I can see the strength
In your will of choices
And that fairytales
Is how your Heart rejoices
But not all of life
Is that clear
Where a man and a woman
Avoids that golden tear
I would like to say
That marriage should come first
But you know that young lovers
Can't avoid their erotic thirst
So why punish
The innocent one
And end his or her life
Before their journey has begun
But who am I
To have a say in the matter
Where I am a man
Who's love has scattered
It is not I
Who has to make that decision
Where a part of my own life
Is under that incision
But I too
Will feel that pain
The moment her choice
Would end a life's game
So I plead
That you change your style of thought
And allow life to flow
Just as time has taught

WALLFLOWER

Then upon the wall
We shall sit and stare
As others dance
Admiring our flare
Even as they dance
We can see their envy
Of the deep feelings
For you I have in me
A wallflower grows
And is destined to bloom
In your wildest dreams
Of the love you shall consume
So we shall wait
Until winter turns to spring
When the wallflower's Heart
Shall forever sing

DEEP IN FLORIDA

Florida is not so far away
My Heart has strayed further
To faithfully prey
But if the distance
Is much to great
For the love you seek
Of a strong black mate
Then Let me know
And I shall end this dream
Of making sweet love to you
Upon the heaven's ravine.

<u>ENDLESS LOVE</u>

My forever woman
My house of love
I look upon the night
And shed a golden tear
Thanks, Thanks, Thanks
You made my life free
You made my Heart sing
Thanks, my forever woman
Love has found me
Love has stolen the night
From man to woman
And woman to man
You are my forever woman
You are my endless love

TEXAS LADY BUG

Somewhere in Texas
Among the soft wind
Gentle
Caressing
I found my Dream
I found my Lady Bug
So innocent
So beautiful
In her eyes
Lies my hopes
In her soul
Lies what makes me a man
Though her Heart
Has been shattered
And abused
There is still love
In this sweet Lady Bug
Somewhere in Texas
I hear her Heartbeat
I feel the essence
Of her tears
To kiss away each broken promise
To make the love
Her body yearns
I shall gladly do
I shall gladly repeat
I shall gladly subdue
Somewhere in Texas
Lies a broken Heart
That is the only Heart
This man seeks
Somewhere in Texas
I found my love
I found my destiny
I found my Lady Bug

<u>LESSONS</u>

I am a good teacher
Even with your two left feet
Of course my lessons
Will make your Heart weak
As each step we take
And each move we make
Will bring out your passion
As your ecstasy faithfully wakes
So come and dance
As your love surrenders
To the deep teachings
Of your one and only HeartSender

VISION

Tell me Queenreena,
Is not the beauty one has inside
That captures a person
With the wonders they hide?
I have a picture
That shows the physical side of me
But it is my mind
That shall satisfy your every fantasy.
Just go to your Guess book
And a vision you shall see
Of the man behind the words
Guiding your destiny

VISION ME

I look at you
So defined
In my awakened dream
I plead to my own desires
Hold back!
Don't let in!
But I can't
I won't!
You have me
Again and again
As a simple picture
Captured me
My DreamGiver
Standing with a smile
Branded upon my mind
Standing with the lips
Branded upon my Heart
My DreamGiver
Look beyond the boundaries
Of these words
Beyond the boundaries
Of your knowledge of love
Search and find
What your Heart seeks
Search and find
Me Loving you
Beyond the physical chambers
Into your deepest passion
Into a place
No other man belongs
My DreamGiver
As your hair dangles
Upon your left breast
It is the grace
Of what is hidden
That stirs my mind
For you hide passion
You hide the want of my love

Close your eyes and vision
Vision the whispering meadows
Vision rolling valleys
Of happy tears
Vision what your destiny holds
DreamGiver
Vision me

<u>MAYBE TOMMORROW</u>

I looked into your eyes
And saw me
Happy
Full of life
The laughter we shared
Yesterday
Fulfilling
You are all I need
But yet,
Am I ready for your love
I am ready?
Can I give the love
You deserve?
You need?
You desire?
A man of dreams
Of passion
Of unending love
This man is yours-
Tomorrow.
Today-
I need your friendship
Your love
Your womanly desire
I need the promise
Of Tomorrow
From you as well
With all of the wonders
I shall give
Maybe Tomorrow
I shall be yours.

But tomorrow never came
From the promise he made
It faded away
From the dawning of the evening shade
She waited and waited
But he never confessed

Of all the Heartache
She now will forever possess
Tomorrow!
Tomorrow!
Damn the Tomorrow!
As now she lives
In eternal sorrow
No one knows
What tomorrow will bring
As now the hounds of pain
Ceases the blooming of Spring
Take a hold of the love
You have at hand
And claim your love
As a strong black man
Don't wait on a promise
Of settling down
Because Maybe Tomorrow
Just won't come around.

<u>OF A POETIC MIND</u>

Well my book is now at the publisher
And soon it will be on display
But if it is poetry you seek
I shall service you without delay
For in my Heart lies a secret
One that should be told
Of love found and love lost
And of memories to forever hold
I use to be a simple man
With goals and many dreams
But now I am so complex
Traveling through life upstream
Pretty Girl, simply open your mind
For a story I shall soon tell
Where two lovers loved deeply
But the walls of their Hearts fell
Who would have thought in this fantasy world
Where life is a big fairytale
That I would find sweet heaven
As my life plunged straight to hell
Being young and ignorant
Is not an excuse to be made
I should have been a man and conquered
The barriers I treacherously layed
For in her eyes and tender soul
I found peace that could not be matched
And in her arms and memorable kiss
I left my own Heart faithfully attached
But things happened
That I would never regret
As we made a young life
And our dreams and goals
Became suspect
Of being banished and unreachable
Even in the light of day
So one of us wanted to escape
While the other dropped to one knee to pray

<u>SATURDAY NIGHT</u>

What else is there to do on a Saturday evening?
Wait a minute I can think of something I would rather
be doing:

> The door bell rings
> A chill
> A thrill
> Anxious as I can be
> My Heartbeat races
> Am I ready for her?
> Is she ready for me?
> We talked a good game
> We teased each other
> But that was phone love
> That was simply words
> Can she back what she said?
> Can I back what she wanted?
>
> I opened the door
> And to my prevail
> An angel appeared
> As her love exhaled
> In simply a smile
> And an overcoat
> My Heart lifted
> And was stuck in my throat
> The desire increased
> And would not cease
> As she whispered to me
> That it was time to release
> I took her gently
> Into my arms
> And promised her
> That I will bring her no harm
> She wanted me
> And the beauty I hold
> I wanted her
> As her passions unfold

Heartsender

Right there
Upon the front door
I pressed against her
As she begged for more
She tugged away
Searching for my manly desire
Knowing that in her
I ignited a fire
As she found
What she was looking for
My bare body
Was now hers to explore
As her coat dropped
And now we were flesh to flesh
I could feel her treasure
Moisten to pass this test
And as I entered
And became overwhelmed
I became the sailor
Leading at the helm
Then deeper and deeper
I went without end
Then louder and louder
My love moved in
As her nails
Found a home in my back
I could sense the neighbors
Wondering who was under attack
But it was I
The victim at hand
Being captured
With a love I couldn't stand
And as my body shook
Deep to her surrender
I was now hers and only her
One and only HeartSender

HUNNIESILK

Excuse me for a moment
As I intrude
Altering Your definition
Not to be rude
But as I vision your picture
I became lost
For your definition
Has not met your beauty's cost
But what I see
Is much much more
Of the ecstasy you promise
As I yearn for more
For you are more than a goddess
That your poem claims
You exceed all boundaries
Of this fantasy game
You lift the tears
Not yet shed
You tame the Heart
Not yet wed
You create a feeling
Not yet felt
And you cause my Heart
To tenderly melt
The mere vision of you
Pauses my eternal time
As I want only you
A victim of love's only crime
But HunnieSilk
Is the name you go by
But in your vision
My love shall forever cry.

<u>MISSING YOU DEEPLY</u>

I woke up the same
Just as the night before
The dream was of you
Once again
Faithfully
I walked around
And saw you
You were at the dining room table
You were sitting on the couch laughing
You were lying on my bed tenderly
You were calling my name from the laundry room
You were everywhere
I walked to your picture
And held you tightly
Kissing you
Wanting you
Over and Over and Over again
But you are far away
Someplace I can't see your smile
Someplace I can't feel the touch of your skin
Someplace I can't kiss your lips
But soon you will be here
Soon I will be with you
Soon I will be making love to you
Soon I will be your forever kind of man
And now I do realize how special you are
How much I need you
How much you brighten my life
And most of all
I do realize just how much
I miss you deeply.

ACROSS THE BROOM

I leap into eternity
Holding your hand
Holding on to life
Across this broom
I confess
I Love you!
I always have
I always will
You brought out in me
Passion
Courage
A desire to succeed
I not only marry you
I marry all that you live for
I marry your smile
I marry your tears
I marry your pain
And your dreams
Across this broom
"I" becomes "We"
"Mine" becomes "Ours"
"Live" becomes "Live For"
I shall be your husband
Not only upon this vow
But upon this soul
And upon this whisper of love
And across this broom
I shall be your Husband
And you shall be my eternal wife
Now and forever

RELEASE!

Then it is time. It is time for you to release the romance you hide. Let your Heart be free and let your passion loose. Imagine yourself with the one you love or the one you will soon love if ever you meet him. Imagine yourself making love to him and giving him all you have in body and in love. Give him everything. Give him your childhood dreams. Give him your deepest secret. Give him a view of your entire body. Let him see every inch of you. Let him touch every spot. Let him memorize each curve. Let him taste each sweet warm forgotten layer of ecstasy you possess. It is time for you to release the tears you hold back from past pain. Let him hold you and kiss away each broken promise and every false vow of love. Make him yours and tell him that no other woman can please him physically or emotionally than the way you can. Just release it. Release the romance you hide and your world will change and you will have control once again of your own Heart just as I have control of the love I have for you.

<u>SHALL WE DANCE</u>

My Dearest Asami
Shall we Dance
This life away
And in each others arms
Forever stay?
Shall we waltz
Into eternity
As our most sensual dream
Becomes reality?
Shall we step
Upon each other's feet
As the whispers of love
Forces our Hearts
To skip a beat?
Shall we spin
Each others world around
Knowing that it is destiny
That we've nomadically found?
Shall we twirl
The laughter upon our tears
As the pain from the past
With time, slowly disappear?
In our dance
There is just you and I
The pedals from the rose
Pure Ecstasy
In our dance
We shall love from down deep
As summer turns to spring
And the winter and autumn
Forever sleeps
Shall we dance
As your Heart, No longer the pretender
As I will always be
Your one and only HeartSender

BREAKFAST

I watched her
Kiss him goodbye
The emptiness
The honorable kiss
I could sense it all
Even as he walked away
She pretended
Dedication
For love
For life
But not for self
What was forced
Has become routine
As he drove away
She waved goodbye
Regretting in Heart
Regretting in her ecstasy
And as the door shut
So did her desire
To be a woman

In the morning light
I come to you
Replacing the lover
You were committed to
In your mind
You know you want me
In your Heart
I am your fantasy
As I enter your realm
Without any delay
Keeping your Heart's promise
As you are now my prey
I prey upon
The gentle spots you hide
As the pleasures I bring
Force tears to your eyes
The emptiness

Of never truly being loved
Will be erased
And all the bad memories
You faithfully embraced
As you open your Heart
To only me
As I bring your dreams
To reality
Over and over
And Over again
I am the one
With the unpure sin
Of loving you
Ever so deep
Of wanting you
To always in your mind keep
Me!
All of Me!
So this breakfast serving
I shall taste
Your treasure
Your forbidden treasure
Your moist unfortold treasure
Over and over
And over again
Deeper and deeper
And even deeper
You shall be mine
Just as I will always be
Your one and only HeartSender

<u>ALWAYS</u>

Shall I give in
And to my Heart
Admit defeat?
Or shall I press on
And to my soul
Strive for my destiny?
You are the one
This I do know
And it is the want of your love
I shall never let go
Many nights
I sat with you on my mind
As I knew nothing
But the curve of your lips
And the tenderness you find
For you are more than a woman,
I want that to be known
You are my dream
And a love I wish to own
Own not as a possession
Yet a feeling I will keep down inside
Loving you in ways
That will keep the tears
From each of your passionate eyes
I know you love another
And it is his Heart you claim
But I am the one
Who's Heart and soul
Shall with you, always remain.

TALENTED ONE

No! You are the talented one
Graceful
Alluring and full of wonders
With thieving eyes
And a tempting smile
A talent that can't be matched
You play upon the emptiness
You dance upon the hopelessness
You sing upon the relentless
Upon your stage
You capture
An audience of souls
As we watch, listen
And dream
Of the passion
You have to give
I applaud your style
Your own vision of love
An agent of laughter
An agent of ecstasy
I long to one day be
For in your arms
You entertain my fears
Of how a love should be
Talented one
I have, I will always
I can never deny
That I am yours.

I AM YOURS

I am yours
I thought you knew
Longing
Waiting
Breathing your scent
Slowing my Heartbeat
Night after night
I stare into the darkness
Thinking of loving you
Stop!
I desperately tell myself
Not to dream of a distant love
But I need you
I want you
I nourish from my desire of you
The silence from your touch
Echoes through my body
No peace
No sanity
No chasing away the tears
I am yours
I have always been yours
Even when I sleep
Your vision claims me
Even when I shower
I think of you
As my body hardens
To the want of you
And the cold water
Becomes boiling hot
Ohhh! If you were here
Showering with me
I would gently cover your body
With the suds from my own body
I would lather you down
As I drop to my knees
And taste your fruits
As I place your thighs

Upon my shoulders
Then deeper and deeper
I taste
Then deeper and deeper
Your nails drive
I would whisper I love you
Deep inside of you
As my tongue dances
The forbidden dance
I could feel your thighs squeeze my head
Come for me!!!
 Are my only thoughts
Let me taste your pleasure
But I wouldn't stop there
No!
I want you to feel me
Now!
With you still in mid air
Against the shower door
You spread yourself
Beggingly
As I enter
Your legs now wrapped
Around my waist
I enter
Slowly
One stroke at a time
The water dances in your hair
As I kiss you deeply
Again you feel me
Deeper are your thoughts
Again you feel me
As your hips begin to roll
Again you feel me
As I could hear your desire scream
Again and Again
And again
Around and around
And around
You roll upon me
There in mid air
As you feel my body muscle

Heartsender

At full strength
Oh God!!!
You scream
Don't Stop!!!
You plead
Damn! I love you!!
I reply
The water is freezing
As we sweat
Creating our own heat
Faster and faster
Deeper and deeper
Upon that door
I could feel your moisture
I could feel your explosion
As we roll
Again and again
Deeper and Deeper
Faster and faster
The screams
From us both
And then
It slows
Yet I am still Inside
I am still stroking
I still have you in arms
But when I open my eyes
You are gone
I was alone
In that shower
Making love to a dream
I can feel the cold water
As I shiver
From wanting you
And then
I knew
That if this were real
And if you were here
There will be no question
To whom I belong
And I now know
That…….

I ....
Am.........
Yours.

AWAY FROM HOME

I feel your pain
That I have caused
And it is true
That I made love
Forever pause

But look deep inside
And feel why it became
A lover's harvest
To a Heartbreaking game

I've seen it in your eyes
Each morning when you awoke
The soft words for another
You never verbally spoke

I kept my pain
Hidden far away
And pretended you loved me
Each night our bodies lay

You thought of him
But made love to me
Sending chaos and sorrow
To my own reality

I should have left
You a long time ago
But each night I prayed
You would let his love go

I nourished from your kiss
And the arms I call home
But soon I began to starve
And was left all alone

Now don`t get me wrong
I have no hate for thee
Just a desire
To see you truly happy

Please let me know
If my perception is oh so wrong
And lead me back to your love
Where I know I belong

<u>OUCH!!</u>

It is painfully
The memory
And then finally
The soft voice
I craved each and every night
It was but a moment
A moment I tend
To always desire
Her voice
Her smile
Her tender eyes
Though she was running late
The brisk conversation
Was all I needed
True love never dies
As time held true
To its undying promise
A fantasy
I shall never again claim
And it hurts so much
It hurts with every Heartbeat
With every muscle
In this strong body
It hurts deeply
That she is not mine
But I have someone
I have someone
I love so much
But why do I still
Cry out for her?
Why do I still deeply
Painfully
Heartstoppingly
Hurt so?

AND THEN THERE IS LOVE

As crazy as life is
There is so much laughter
And so many memories
To carry in the ever after
There are the rolling waves
And dancing storms
Challenging your dreams
Since the day you were born
An Autumn's cry
As the leaves begin to fall
A babies curiosity
As their smiles begin to crawl
A deer in flight
Running for a place to hide
As the hunters prey
Upon the arrow in it's side

And then there is love
Unexplainable
Without boundaries
I slept the night
In fear
When I awake
Will love be there?
We argued
Just as we did before
Except this time
It was I
Who had to even the score
I should not have said
The words that just flowed
I should have held back
My cruel senseless attack

And then there is love
I knew her so well
As she laid in my arms
Under my whispering spell

Heartsender

We danced the night away
Once again and again
She knew it was only her
Who had my love to win
I know now
That she is the one for me
And I shall love her
For all of eternity

And then there is love
Why! Why! Why!
Did she hurt me so
Time and time again!
I must let this love go!
For no reason
Her anger stole the scene
Making her point
In my broken Heart's ravine
I tried
But she will never change
The love she tends to give
Is far too sometimingly strange.

And then there is love
I am so glad I have you
To hold and cherish
These nights through
You mean so much
To the life I live
I just wish I'll always have you
With love to always give

And then there is love
Even with the ups and downs
I know that in my Heart
I want for you to always be around
And then there is love

March 21, 2000

<u>SUNRISE</u>

Unforgettable vision
Passing upon the moments
Unforgettable passion
Falling, falling, falling
A birth of light
Of fire from within
A birth of life
Of new and everlasting
Rising from Dark waters
Made of unwanted tears
Passing clouds
Passing sparrows
Passing time
And
The beginning...Is it?